THE
SHACK

STUDY GUIDE

Healing for Your Journey through Loss,
Trauma, and Pain

WM. PAUL YOUNG
&
BRAD ROBISON, M.D.

windblown
MEDIA
Newbury Park, California

Scriptures marked MSG are from *The Message.* Copyright © 1993, 1994, 1995, 1996, 2000, 2001, 2002. Used by permission of NavPress Publishing Group.

The authors are represented by Ambassador Literary Agency, Nashville, TN, and Baxter/Stinson/Polk, Annapolis, MD.

Quotes taken from *The Shack* published by Windblown Media
4680 Calle Norte
Newbury Park, CA 91320

Published in association with Hachette Book Group
1290 Avenue of the Americas
New York, NY 10104
hachettebookgroup.com

Printed in the United States of America

First Edition: November 2016
10 9 8 7 6 5

The publisher is not responsible for websites (or their content) that are not owned by the publisher.

ISBN 978-1-4555-9791-8

CONTENTS

INTRODUCTION

Thank you for your interest in this study guide, which we trust will serve as an experiential guide through a healing process in your life. We have all been impacted and hurt by the disease, dysfunction, and destruction of this broken world. All of us are in need of healing and restoration. Every intentional movement toward wholeness is connected to relationship, to spiritual friendship, and to the discovery of the beauty God has created within *you*, within *your* humanity, and within *your* community.

This guide is meant to help you experience the presence of the triune God, not in some cathedral or stronghold of your own making, but in "the shack" of your deepest pain. It is there that you will be confronted and comforted with the real relational truth of who God is and who you are. It is there that you will find your way, in grace and truth, deeper into a life filled with healthy affiliations. The invitation is to exchange self-protective isolation for life-giving solitude and openness to community that will lead *you* to the festival of friends.

You can use this study guide in several ways. You can work through it on your own for personal healing, as a part of a small group/book club, or even during a weekend retreat. The chapter numbers and titles are identical to those found in the book, *The Shack*. For maximum benefit, you will read the chapter from *The Shack*, and then you will work your way through the corresponding chapter in this guide.

Many of the questions are personal, so if you use this guide in a group setting or on a retreat, please practice caregiving. Courtesy and mutual respect lay the foundation for any healthy group. A small group should be a safe place for all who participate. Respect the confidentiality of the person who is sharing. What they share may be highly sensitive in nature and sometimes controversial. Small group intimacy is not fodder for gossip, but an invitation to participate in authentic community. A small group is not a place to tell others what they should have done or said or think, or to force opinions on others. Commit yourselves to listening to one another, be sensitive to all perspectives, and show others the grace you would like to receive yourself.

Remember, you or a group member may be carrying a "great sadness" from severe trauma or loss that happened in your "shack." As authors of this guide, we, but more importantly Papa, invite you to join Him on a healing journey through *The Shack*.

It's been a while. I've missed you.
I'll be at the shack next weekend if you want to get together.

—PAPA

FOREWORD

Hurtful and Healing Relationships

I SUPPOSE THAT since most of our hurts come through relationships, so will our healing.

1. Whether you believe there is a God or not, reflect for a moment on what it would be like to spend the weekend with God face-to-face.

2. What is it like to "hang out" with a friend?

3. How would they be alike? How would they be different?

FOR ALMOST TWO days, tied to the big oak at the back of the house, he was beaten with a belt and Bible verses every time his dad woke from a stupor and put down his bottle.

4. **Write your reflections on this passage and Mack's early life experiences.**

IN A WORLD of talkers, Mack is a thinker and doer. He doesn't say much unless you ask him directly, which most folks have learned not to do. When he does speak you wonder if he isn't some sort of alien who sees the landscape of human ideas and experiences differently than everybody else.

The thing is, he usually makes uncomfortable sense in a world where most folks would rather just hear what they are used to hearing, which is often not much of anything. Those who know him generally like him well enough, provided he keeps his thoughts mostly to himself. And when he does talk, it isn't that they stop liking him—rather, they are not quite so satisfied with themselves.

Mack once told me that he used to speak his mind more freely in his younger years, but he admitted that most of such talk was a survival mechanism to cover his hurts; he often ended up spewing his pain on everyone around him. He says that he had a way of pointing out people's faults and humiliating them while maintaining his own sense of false power and control. Not too endearing.

5. **Reflect on who Mack is. How does he cope? How has that evolved over time?**

MACK HAS BEEN married to Nan for just more than thirty-three mostly happy years. He says she saved his life and paid a high price to do it. For some reason beyond understanding, she seems to love him now more than ever, even though I get the sense that he hurt her something fierce in the early years. I suppose that since most of our hurts come through relationships, so will our healing, and I know that grace rarely makes sense for those looking in from the outside.

6. Reflect on where most of our hurts and healing come from.

AND WITH RESPECT to God, Mack is no longer just wide, he has gone way deep. But the dive cost him dearly.

These days are very different from seven or so years ago, when *The Great Sadness* entered his life and he almost quit talking altogether.

7. Is your relationship with God wide, deep, both, or neither?

Reflect on *The Great Sadness*.

You know that place: where there is just you alone—and maybe God, if you believe in him. Of course, God might be there even if you *don't* believe in him. That would be just like him. He hasn't been called the Grand Interferer for nothing.

8. **Reflect on your internal world, "that place: where there is just you alone—and maybe God."**

What you are about to read is something that Mack and I have struggled with for many months to put into words. It's a little, well...no, it is a *lot* on the fantastic side. Whether some parts of it are actually true or not, I won't be the judge. Suffice it to say that while some things may not be scientifically provable, they can still be true nonetheless. I will tell you honestly that being a part of this story has affected me deep inside, in places I had never been before and didn't even know existed; I confess to you that I desperately want everything Mack has told me to be true. Most days I am right there with him, but on others—when the visible world of concrete and computers seems to be the *real* world—I lose touch and have my doubts.

9. **Reflect on truth and the *real* world.**

A CONFLUENCE OF PATHS

Storms, Falls, Letters, God, and a Great Sadness

1. Reflect on the intrusions (big or small, internal or external, pleasant or tragic) in your life. How do you react to those intrusions?

THERE IS SOMETHING joyful about storms that interrupt routine. Snow or freezing rain suddenly releases you from expectations, performance demands, and the tyranny of appointments and schedules. And unlike illness, it is largely a corporate rather than individual experience. One can almost hear a unified sigh rise from the nearby city and surrounding countryside where Nature has intervened to give respite to the weary humans slogging it out within her purview. All those affected this way are united by a mutual excuse, and the heart is suddenly and unexpectedly a little giddy. There will be no apologies needed for not showing up to some commitment or other. Everyone understands and shares in this singular justification, and the sudden alleviation of the pressure to produce makes the heart merry.

2. Reflect on this type of intrusion and the pressure to produce.

EVEN COMMONPLACE ACTIVITIES become extraordinary. Routine choices become adventures and are often experienced with a sense of heightened clarity.

   3. **Reflect on intrusive storms in your life that have caused common-place activities to become extraordinary adventures.**

IT WAS A glorious world and for a brief moment its blazing splendor almost lifted, even if only for a few seconds, *The Great Sadness* from Mack's shoulders.

   4. **Reflections.**

MACKENZIE,
It's been **a** while. I've missed you.
I'll be at the shack next weekend if you want to get together.
                                        —Papa

   Mack stiffened as a wave of nausea rolled over him and then just as quickly mutated into anger. He purposely thought about the shack as little as possible, and even when he did, his thoughts were neither kind nor good. If this was someone's idea of a bad joke, he had truly outdone himself. And to sign it "Papa" just made it all the more horrifying.

   5. **Reflect on these types of intrusions and unexpected triggers of strong emotion.**

THERE WAS OFTEN some compensation in every trial, if one looked hard enough.

6. **Reflect on the little and big trials or intrusions in your life and those around you. Do you agree or disagree with the above statement?**

"**NOW ANNIE, YOU** know I don't smoke dope—never did, and don't ever want to." Of course Annie knew no such thing, but Mack was taking no chances on how she might remember the conversation in a day or two. Wouldn't be the first time that her sense of humor morphed into a good story that soon became "fact." He could see his name being added to the church prayer chain. "It's okay, I'll just catch Tony some other time, no big deal."

7. **Reflect on this type of intrusion and how Mack is responding.**

"**MACK, I WISH** I knew. She is just like talking to a rock, and no matter what I do I can't get through. When we're around family she seems to come out of her shell some, but then she disappears again. I just don't know what to do. I've been praying and praying that Papa would help us find a way to reach her, but"—she paused again—"it feels like he isn't listening."

8. **Reflect on Katie's shell.**

Reflect on Papa and your own experience of God.

Does God listen?

THE GATHERING DARK

The Secret Places of Your Heart

Nothing makes us so lonely as our secrets.
—PAUL TOURNIER

1. Reflect on the secrets of your life and the inner workings of your heart and mind.

2. What has shaped your heart and mind the most?

LITTLE DISTRACTIONS LIKE the ice storm were a welcome although brief respite from the haunting presence of his constant companion: *The Great Sadness*, as he referred to it. Shortly after the summer that Missy vanished, *The Great Sadness* had draped itself around Mack's shoulders like some invisible but almost tangibly heavy quilt. The weight of its presence dulled his eyes and stooped his shoulders. Even his efforts to shake it off were exhausting, as if his arms were sewn into its bleak folds of despair and he had somehow become part of it. He ate, worked, loved, dreamed and played in this garment of heaviness, weighed down as if he were wearing a leaden bathrobe—trudging daily through the murky despondency that sucked the color out of everything.

3. Reflect on what Mack is going through.

4. What has draped itself around you?

OTHER TIMES HE would dream that his feet were stuck in cloying mud as he caught brief glimpses of Missy running down the wooded path ahead of him, her red cotton summer dress gilded with wildflowers flashing among the trees. She was completely oblivious to the dark shadow tracking her from behind. Although he frantically tried to scream warnings to her, no sound emerged and he was always too late and too impotent to save her. He would bolt upright in bed, sweat dripping from his tortured body, while waves of nausea and guilt and regret rolled over him like some surreal tidal flood.

5. Consider Mack's experience in this passage. Look specifically at the thoughts, feelings, and physical symptoms associated with his intrusive images and nightmares.

6. Do not linger here if you are not ready, but at least let yourself be aware of any intrusive dreams, images, thoughts, feelings, and physical symptoms that you experience.

THE STORY OF Missy's disappearance is, unfortunately, not unlike others told too often.

7. Missy's story, Paul Young's story, and your story of trauma or loss are, unfortunately, all too common. When you are ready, write down your story. Consider sharing your story, but only with someone who has consistently proven to be a safe and reliable person.

...THE LEGEND OF the beautiful Indian maid, the daughter of a chief of the Multnomah tribe.... Missy usually loved the telling, almost as much as Mack did. It had all the elements of a true redemption story, not unlike the story of Jesus that she knew so well. It centered on a father who loved his only child and a sacrifice foretold by a prophet. Because of love, the child willingly gave up her life to save her betrothed and their tribes from certain death.

8. Allow yourself to reflect openly and honestly on redemptive stories even if all you feel is hurt, anger, or disbelief.

THAT EVENING, AS he sat among three laughing children watching one of nature's greatest shows, Mack's heart was suddenly penetrated by unexpected joy. A sunset of brilliant colors and patterns played off the few clouds that had waited in the wings to become central actors in this unique presentation. He was a rich man, he thought to himself, in all the ways that mattered.

9. **Reflect on past, present, and future joys. During this journey, do not try to manufacture emotions or experiences, but let yourself be penetrated by all that you experience.**

BEFORE IT GOT too late, the four went on a short hike away from the campfires and lanterns, to a dark and quiet spot where they could lie down and gaze in wonder at the Milky Way, stunning and intense when undiminished by the pollution of city lights. Mack could lie and gaze up into that vastness for hours. He felt so incredibly small yet comfortable with himself. Of all the places he sensed the presence of God, out here, surrounded by nature and under the stars, was one of the most tangible.

10. **Where is the presence of God most tangible to you? Even if you are not sure you believe in God, reflect on moments of transcendent presence with you in the past and be open to experience that presence during this journey.**

"DADDY, HOW COME she had to die?... Did the Indian princess really die? Is the story true?"

Mack thought before he spoke. "I don't know, Kate. It's a legend, and sometimes legends are stories that teach a lesson."

"So, it didn't really happen?" asked Missy.

"It might have, sweetie. Sometimes legends are built from real stories, things that really happen."

Again silence, then, "So is Jesus dying a legend?"

Mack could hear the wheels turning in Kate's mind. "No, honey, that's a true story. And do you know what? I think the Indian princess story is probably true too."

Mack waited while his girls processed their thoughts.

Missy was next to ask, "Is the Great Spirit another name for God—you know, Jesus' Papa?"

Mack smiled in the dark. Obviously, Nan's nightly prayers were having an effect. "I would suppose so. It's a good name for God because he is a spirit and he is great."

"Then how come he's so *mean*?"

11. Reflections.

12. Why is God so *mean*?

During this journey be open to not only the question of whether there is a God, but also to the question of who or what God is. You may find that there are competing thoughts, feelings, and beliefs on this subject inside you.

"**SWEETHEART, JESUS DIDN'T** think his Daddy was mean. He thought his Daddy was full of love and loved him very much. His Daddy didn't *make* him die. Jesus chose to die because he and his Daddy love you and me and everyone in the world. He saved us from our sickness, just like the princess."

13. Reflections.

During this journey, question God, be angry with God, but most of all be honest with yourself and God. Let this process expose all the secret places of your heart and entertain the possibility that you just might experience a God who loves you, is with you, and is healing you.

THE TIPPING POINT

The Thoughts, Emotions, and Core Beliefs of the Past and the Future

1. As you read this chapter and the rest of the book, reflect. Reflect on the past and the future, but most of all reflect on and be present in the moment. Reflect on, sift, and separate thoughts, feelings, and core beliefs that rise to the surface of your heart and mind. Let these questions be your guide not your task.

(Don't spend too much time on points 2–4 right now, but at least begin the process of sifting and separating thoughts, emotions, core beliefs, identity, and behavior. And be open to emotional and spiritual growth.)

2. Consider the differences between thoughts, emotions, and core beliefs.

3. How do thoughts, emotions, and core beliefs combine to make you who you are?

4. How do thoughts, emotions, and core beliefs drive behavior and shape growth?

THIS IS ONE of those rare and precious moments, thought Mack, *that catches you by surprise and almost takes your breath away. If only Nan could be here, it truly would be perfect.*

5. **Reflect on and share some of your precious perfect moments. (Be aware of how these reflections on the past influence your thoughts, emotions, and beliefs in the present.)**

"SHE HELPS PEOPLE think through their relationship with God in the face of their own death," Mack answered.

"I'd love to hear more about that," encouraged Jesse as he stirred up the fire with a stick, causing it to bloom with renewed vigor.

Mack hesitated. As much as he felt unusually at ease with these two, he didn't really know them, and the conversation had gotten a little deeper than he was comfortable with. He searched quickly for a short answer to Jesse's interest.

"Nan's a lot better at that than I am. I guess she thinks about God differently than most folks. She even calls him Papa because of the closeness of their relationship, if that makes sense."

"Of course it does!" exclaimed Sarah as Jesse nodded. "Is that a family thing, referring to God as Papa?"

"No," said Mack, laughing. "The kids have picked it up some, but I'm not comfortable with it. It just seems a little too familiar for me. Anyway, Nan has a wonderful father, so I think it's just easier for her."

It had slipped out, and Mack inwardly shuddered, hoping no one had noticed, but Jesse was looking right at him. "Your dad wasn't too wonderful?" he asked gently.

"Yeah." Mack paused. "I guess you could say he was not too wonderful. He died when I was just a kid, of natural causes." Mack laughed, but the sound was empty. He looked at the two. "He drank himself to death."

6. **Reflect on not only the content of this passage but also the experience of opening up to someone. What makes opening up easy or hard?**

HE BREWED HIS final nightly cup of coffee and sat sipping it in front of the fire that had burned itself down to a flickering mass of red-hot coals. It was so easy to get lost inside such a bed of glowing undulating embers. He was alone, yet not alone. Wasn't that a line from the Bruce Cockburn song "Rumors of Glory"? He wasn't sure, but if he remembered he would look it up when he got home.

As he sat mesmerized by the fire and wrapped in its warmth, he prayed, mostly prayers of thanksgiving. He had been given so much. *Blessed* was probably the right word. He was content, at rest, and full of peace.

7. **Reflect on your quiet times when you are alone, yet not alone. Are you content, at rest, full of peace?**

Ponder times when you are and when you are not. How much of the past or the future intrudes into your present?

MACK DID NOT know it then, but within twenty-four hours his prayers would change, drastically.

...It is remarkable how a seemingly insignificant action or event can change entire lives. Kate, lifting her paddle to wave back in response, lost her balance and tipped the canoe. There was a frozen look of terror on her face as almost in silence and slow motion it rolled over. Josh frantically leaned to try to balance, but it was too late and he disappeared from sight in the midst of the splash. Mack was already headed for the water's edge, not intending to go in but to be near when they bobbed up. Kate was up first, sputtering and crying, but there was no sign of Josh. Then suddenly, an eruption of water and legs, and Mack knew instantly that something was terribly wrong.

8. **Have things in life changed in an instant? Write down a few thoughts.**

MACK SURFACED, YELLED at Kate to swim to shore, gulped what air he could, and went under a second time. By his third dive and knowing time was running out, Mack realized that he could either keep trying to free Josh from the vest or flip the canoe. Since Josh in his panic was not letting anyone near him, Mack chose the latter. Whether it was God and angels or God and adrenaline, he would never know for sure, but on only his second attempt he succeeded in rolling the canoe over, freeing Josh from his tether.

The jacket, finally able to do what it was designed for, now kept the boy's face up above water. Mack surfaced behind Josh, who now was limp and unconscious, blood oozing from a gash on his head where the canoe had banged him as Mack had righted it. He immediately began mouth-to-mouth on his son as best he could, while others, who had heard the commotion, arrived to pull him and the canoe with the attached vest toward the shallows.

Oblivious to the shouts around him as people barked instructions and questions, Mack focused on his task, his own panic building inside his chest. Just as his feet touched solid ground, Josh began to cough and throw up water and breakfast. A huge cheer erupted from everyone gathered, but Mack couldn't have cared less. Overwhelmed with relief and the adrenaline rush of a narrow escape, he began to cry, and then suddenly Kate was sobbing with her arms around his neck, and everyone was laughing and crying and hugging.

9. **When your life changed in an instant, what were the circumstances? Write out a moment by moment timeline of what happened.**

What were your emotions?

How much do those thoughts, emotions, and images intrude into your present moment, or how hard do you have to work to keep them out of your present?

THE GREAT SADNESS

The Initial Stages of Trauma and Loss

As you work through this process, be intentional about it,
but don't rush it. Take short breaks, especially between chapters.
Don't let the healing process slow too much, but give it time.

1. What stood out to you in the last chapter?

2. What were the emotions that you felt as you read?

SIX SHOWER STALLS and no Missy. He checked the men's toilet stalls and showers, trying not to think about why he would even bother looking there. She was nowhere and he jogged back toward Emil's, unable to pray anything except, "Oh, God, help me find her...Oh, God, please help me find her."

3. Reflect on Mack's emotions at this point. Reflect on fear and your experience of it.

IT WAS SLOW, methodical work, much too slow for Mack, but he knew that this was the most logical way to find her if...if she was still on the campgrounds. As he walked between tents and trailers, he was praying and promising. He knew in his heart that promising things to God was rather dumb and irrational, but he couldn't help it. He was desperate to get Missy back, and surely God knew where she was.

4. Reflect on this passage and your experience of similar moments.

WHAT HE WOULD give for a do-over: a chance to have this day start from the beginning.

5. What are the "do-overs" that keep running through your mind?

AS HE LISTENED to Dalton's conversation with Special Agent Wikowsky, Mack felt the last of his hope draining away. He slumped to the ground and buried his face in his hands. Was there ever a man as tired as he was at this moment? For the first time since Missy's disappearance, he allowed himself to consider the range of horrendous possibilities, and once it started he couldn't stop; the imaginations of good and evil all mixed up together in a soundless but terrifying parade. Even when he tried to shake free of the images, he couldn't. Some were horrible ghastly snapshots of torture and pain: of monsters and demons of the deepest dark with barbwire fingers and razor touches; of Missy screaming for her daddy and no one answering. And mixed throughout these horrors were flashes of other memories: the toddler with her Missy-sippy cup as they had called it; the two-year-old drunk from eating too much chocolate cake; and the one image so recently made as she fell asleep safely in her daddy's arms. Unyielding images. What would he say at her funeral? What could he possibly say to Nan? How could this have happened? God, how could this happen?

6. **Reflect on this situation, Mack's thoughts and emotions. Then reflect on your own experience of intrusive thoughts, emotions, and images. (I want to emphasis here the importance of reflection. Don't just think about these things; reflect, set with the emotions and images, then think and write out what you are experiencing.)**

...HE WAS SWEPT helplessly away in the unrelenting and merciless grip of growing despair, slowly rocking back and forth. Soul-shredding sobs and groans clawed to the surface from the core of his being.

7. **Reflect on despair.**

IN ONE DAY he had spent a year's worth of emotions, and now he felt numb, adrift in a suddenly meaningless world that felt like it would be forever gray.

8. **Consider the emotion of numb. What is its purpose? How does it function?**

JESSE AND SARAH, willing to do anything, made themselves constantly available to the family and friends who came to help. They lifted the huge burden of communication with the public from both Nan and Mack and seemed to be everywhere as they skillfully wove some threads of peace into the turbulence of emotions.

9. Reflect on "skillfully wove some threads of peace into the turbulence of emotions." Reflect on peace. How is it different than numb?

IT SEEMED THAT all who spoke, regardless of their point of view, were deeply affected by the situation. Something in the hearts of most human beings simply cannot abide pain inflicted on the innocent, especially children. Even broken men serving in the worst correctional facilities will often first take out their own rage on those who have caused suffering to children. Even in such a world of relative morality, causing harm to a child is still considered absolutely wrong. Period!

10. Reflect on morality and "absolute wrong."

IT TOOK MACK'S crew almost three hours to reach the first team and by then it was all over. The dogs had done the rest, uncovering a descending game trail that led more than a mile into a small hidden valley. There they found a run-down little shack near the edge of a pristine lake barely half a mile across, fed by a cascading creek a hundred yards away. A century or so earlier this had probably been a settler's home. It had two good-sized rooms, enough to house a small family. Since that time, it had most likely served as an occasional hunter's or poacher's cabin.

11. Consider the significance of this place for Mack at this point.

ON THE FLOOR by the fireplace lay Missy's torn and blood-soaked red dress.

12. Reflect on Mack's and your own emotions triggered by this scene.

FOR MACK, THE next few days and weeks became a numbing blur of interviews with law enforcement and the press, followed by a memorial service for Missy with a small empty coffin and an endless sea of faces, all sad as they paraded by, no one knowing what to say. Sometime during the weeks that followed, Mack began the slow and painful trek back into everyday life.

13. Reflect on this part of the grief process and the "slow and painful trek back into everyday life."

ALTHOUGH NO ONE involved was left unmarked by the tragedy, Kate seemed to have been affected the most, disappearing into a shell, like a turtle protecting its soft underbelly from anything potentially dangerous. It seemed that she would poke her head out only when she felt fully safe, which was becoming less and less often. Mack and Nan both worried increasingly about her but couldn't seem to find the right words to penetrate the fortress she was building around her heart. Attempts at conversation would turn into one-way monologues, with sounds bouncing off her stone visage. It was as if something had died inside her, and now was slowly infecting her from the inside, spilling out occasionally in bitter words or emotionless silence.

Josh fared much better, due in part to the long-distance relationship he had kept up with Amber. E-mail and the telephone gave him an outlet for his pain, and she had given him the time and space to grieve. He was also preparing to graduate from high school with all the distractions that his senior year provided.

The Great Sadness had descended and in differing degrees cloaked everyone whose life had touched Missy's. Mack and Nan weathered the storm of loss together with reasonable success, and in some ways they were closer for it. Nan had made it clear from the start, and repeatedly, that she did not blame Mack in any way for what happened. Understandably, it took Mack much longer to let himself off the hook, even a little bit.

14. **Consider how each individual coped with the loss of Missy. How do you think you and those around you would cope or have coped with trauma or loss?**

IT IS SO easy to get sucked into the if-only game, and playing it is a short and slippery slide into despair.

15. **Reflect on "what if"s, "if only"s, and the "slippery slide into despair."**

THE TRAGEDY HAD also increased the rift in Mack's own relationship with God, but he ignored this growing sense of separation. Instead, he tried to embrace a stoic, unfeeling faith, and even though Mack found some comfort and peace in that, it didn't stop the nightmares where his feet were stuck in the mud and his soundless screams could not save his precious Missy. The bad dreams were becoming less frequent, and laughter and moments of joy were slowly returning, but he felt guilty about these.

So when Mack received the note from "Papa" telling him to meet him back at the shack, it was no small event. Does God even write notes? And why *the shack*—the icon of his deepest pain? Certainly God would have better places to meet with him. A dark thought even crossed his mind that the killer could be taunting him or luring him away to leave the rest of his family unprotected. Maybe it was all just a cruel hoax. But then why was it signed "Papa"?

16. Look at Mack's relationship with God and the statement "stoic, un-feeling faith."

How would you describe your faith before and after trauma?

Where does God meet you? Listen, look for, and respond to God's invitation to join you in the place of your deepest pain.

TRY AS HE might, Mack could not escape the desperate possibility that the note just might be from God after all, even if the thought of God passing notes did not fit well with his theological training. In seminary he had been taught that God had completely stopped any overt communication with moderns, preferring to have them only listen to and follow sacred Scripture, properly interpreted, of course. God's voice had been reduced to paper, and even that paper had to be moderated and deciphered by the proper authorities and intellects. It seemed that direct communication with God was something exclusively for the ancients and uncivilized, while educated Westerners' access to God was mediated and controlled by the intelligentsia. Nobody wanted God in a box, just in a book. Especially an expensive one bound in leather with gilt edges, or was that guilt edges?

17. Reflections.

BUT IN SPITE of his anger and depression, Mack knew that he needed some answers. He realized he was stuck, and Sunday prayers and hymns weren't cutting it anymore, if they ever really had. Cloistered spirituality seemed to change nothing in the lives of the people he knew, except maybe Nan. But she was special. God might really love her. She wasn't a screwup like him. He was sick of God and God's religion, sick of all the little religious social clubs that didn't seem to make any real difference or affect any real changes. Yes, Mack wanted more, and he was about to get much more than he bargained for.

18. Reflections.

GUESS WHO'S COMING TO DINNER

Facts, Reason, and Logic

1. What stood out to you in the last chapter?

2. What were the emotions that you felt as you read the last chapter?

THERE ARE TIMES when you choose to believe something that would normally be considered absolutely irrational. It doesn't mean that it is *actually* irrational, but it surely is not rational. Perhaps there is suprarationality: reason beyond the normal definitions of fact or data-based logic; something that makes sense only if you can see a bigger picture of reality. Maybe that is where faith fits in.

3. What is faith?

4. Where does faith fit into facts, reason, and logic?

"I AM KEEPING it to myself for *Nan's* sake," he told himself. Besides, acknowledging the note would mean admitting that he had kept secrets from her; secrets he still justified in his own mind. Sometimes honesty can be incredibly messy.

5. Why do we keep things hidden inside sometimes?

6. Reflect on honesty, secrets, and things we keep hidden.

"I'M NOT SURE, Willie. I guess part of me would like to believe that God would care enough about me to send a note. I'm so confused, even after all this time. I just don't know what to think and it isn't getting better. I feel like we're losing Kate, and that's killing me. Maybe what happened to Missy is God's judgment for what I did to my own dad. I just don't know." He looked up into the face of a man who cared more about him than anyone he knew, except Nan. "All I know is that I need to go back."

7. Consider what Mack is going through.

The reasons you are working through this study guide right now
may feel just as confusing as Mack's struggle. Trust that God did invite
you on this journey and resolve yourself to go.

THERE WAS SILENCE between them before Willie spoke again. "So, when do we leave?"

Mack was touched by his friend's willingness to jump into his insanity.

8. Reflect on the people in your life who are willing to jump into your insanity.

"SO, WHAT DO you think he looks like?" Willie chuckled as he approached.

"Who?" asked Mack.

"God, of course. What do you think he'll look like, if he even bothers to show up, I mean? Boy, I can just see you scaring the living daylights out of some poor hiker—asking him if he's God and then demanding answers an' all."

9. What does God look like to you?

HE RETRACED THE same path they had taken three and a half years before, with a few minor changes: not as many potty breaks, and he sailed by Multnomah Falls without looking. He had pushed away any thoughts of the place since Missy's disappearance, sequestering his emotions securely in the padlocked basement of his own heart.

10. Reflect on how emotions and the heart operate. Allow yourself to be aware of the places in your heart that have padlocks on them.

HIS EYES DARKENED and his hands tightened on the steering wheel as he fought the temptation at every off-ramp to turn around and go home. He knew he was driving straight into the center of his pain, the vortex of *The Great Sadness* that had so diminished his sense of being alive. Flashes of visual memory and stabbing instants of blistering fury now came in waves, attended by the taste of bile and blood in his mouth.

11. **Reflect on what Mack is going through. Allow yourself to "drive straight into the center of your pain," the vortex of your *Great Sadness*.**

THE PAIN THAT had been building in his stomach finally pushed him into panic. After only five steps, he stopped and retched so strongly that it brought him to his knees.

"Please help me!" he groaned. He stood up on shaky legs and took another step away from the car. Then he stopped and turned back. He opened the passenger door and reached in, rummaging around until he felt the small tin box. He pried the lid off and found what he was looking for, his favorite picture of Missy, which he removed along with the note. Replacing the lid, he left the box on the seat.

12. **Reflect. Take time to find the objects that give you courage and strength for this journey.**

MACK THE COURAGEOUS had been reduced to just another scared boy in the woods. Snapping the safety back on, he tucked the gun away. *Someone could get hurt,* he thought with a sigh of relief.

13. **Reflect. Take time to step away from the things that may give you a false sense of safety but may actually be destructive (alcohol, drugs, promiscuity, self-injury). Do not rely on those things to get you through this journey. If those things worsen as you continue, seek help from healthy trusted support.**

TAKING ANOTHER DEEP breath and exhaling slowly, he calmed himself. Determined that he was done being afraid, he continued down the path, trying to look more confident than he felt. He hoped he hadn't come all this way for nothing. If God was really meeting him here, he was more than ready to get a few things off his chest, respectfully, of course.

14. **Reflect on finding the courage to face God in your pain versus trying to hide your emotions and pain from God.**

A FEW TURNS later he stumbled out of the woods and into a clearing. At the far side and down the slope he saw it—the shack.

15. **Reflect on what the shack meant for Mack, and what it represents for you.**

I'M SO SORRY, honey. Tears began to well up in his eyes.

And finally his heart exploded like a flash flood, releasing his pent-up anger and letting it rush down the rocky canyons of his emotions. Turning his eyes heavenward, he began screaming his anguished questions. "Why? Why did you let this happen? Why did you bring me here? Of all the places to meet you—why *here*? Wasn't it enough to kill my baby? Do you have to toy with me too?"

In a blind rage, Mack grabbed the nearest chair and flung it at the window. It smashed into pieces. He picked up one of the legs and began destroying everything he could. Groans and moans of despair and fury burst through his lips as he beat his wrath into the terrible place. "I hate you!" In a frenzy he pounded out his rage until he was exhausted and spent.

16. **Reflect on what Mack is going through and your own rage. Do you ever let that rage be directed at God? Why or why not?**

EVEN IN HIS exhaustion the anger seethed, and he once again took aim at the indifferent God he imagined somewhere beyond the roof of the shack. "God, you couldn't even let us find her and bury her properly. Was that just too much to ask?"

17. **Reflect on "the indifferent God."**

AS THE MIX of emotions ebbed and flowed, his anger giving way to pain, a fresh wave of sorrow began to mix with his confusion. "So where are you? I thought you wanted to meet me here. Well, I'm here, God. And you? You're nowhere to be found! You've never been around when I've needed you—not when I was a little boy, not when I lost Missy. Not now! Some 'Papa' you are!" He spat out the words.

Mack sat there in silence, the *emptiness* of the place invading his soul. His jumble of unanswered questions and far-flung accusations settled to the floor with him, and then slowly drained into a pit of desolation. *The Great Sadness* tightened around him, and he almost welcomed the smothering sensation. *This* pain he knew. He was familiar with it, almost like a friend.

18. Reflect on Mack's anger at God and the pit of desolation. Is there a link?

KILLING HIMSELF WOULD be one way to strike back at God, if God even existed.

Clouds parted outside, and a sunbeam suddenly spilled into the room, piercing the center of his despair. But...what about Nan? And what about Josh and Kate and Tyler and Jon? As much as he longed to stop the ache in his heart, he knew he could not add to their hurt.

19. Reflect. When you are ready, look around for a sunbeam piercing the center of your despair and the people whose hurt you do not want to add to.

HE LOOKED UP into the open rafters. "I'm done, God," he whispered. "I can't do this anymore. I'm tired of trying to find you in all of this." And with that, he walked out the door. Mack determined that this was the last time he would go looking for God. If God wanted him, God would have to come find him.

20. Do you ever get tired of trying to find God? Is it possible that the God you were expecting to find does not exist? Maybe it is time to let God find you.

MACK WAS NO longer thinking about home. A terror gripped him, as if he had opened Pandora's box and was being swept away into the center of madness, to be lost forever. Unsteady, he carefully turned around, trying to hold on to some sense of sanity.

...Perhaps this was what it was like to experience a complete psychotic break. "I'm losing it," Mack whispered to himself. "This can't be happening. This isn't real."

21. Have you ever had experiences with God that you initially thought,
    This can't be real?

HE NOW FACED another dilemma. What should you do when you come to the door of a house, or cabin in this case, where God might be? Should you knock? Presumably God already knew that Mack was there. Maybe he ought to simply walk in and introduce himself, but that seemed equally absurd. And how should he address him? Should he call him "Father," or "Almighty One," or perhaps "Mr. God," and would it be best if he fell down and worshiped? Not that he was really in the mood.

22. Reflect on Mack's dilemma. What do you call God, and why?

AS HE TRIED to establish some inner mental balance, the anger that he thought had so recently died inside him began to emerge. No longer concerned or caring about what to call God and energized by his ire, he walked up to the door. Mack decided to bang loudly and see what happened, but just as he raised his fist to do so, the door flew open, and he was looking directly into the face of a large, beaming African-American woman.

Instinctively he jumped back, but he was too slow. With speed that belied her size, she crossed the distance between them and engulfed him in her arms, lifting him clear off his feet and spinning him around like a little child. And all the while she was shouting his name—"Mackenzie Allen Phillips"—with the ardor of someone seeing a long-lost and deeply loved relative. She finally put him back on Earth and, with her hands on his shoulders, pushed him back as if to get a good look at him.

"Mack, look at you!" she fairly exploded. "Here you are, and so grown up. I have really been looking forward to seeing you face-to-face. It is so wonderful to have you here with us. My, my, my, how I do love you!" And with that she wrapped herself around him again.

23. Consider Mack's anger, expectations, and experience in this situation.

MACK WAS SPEECHLESS. In a few seconds this woman had breached pretty much every social propriety behind which he had so safely entrenched himself.

…He could feel the warmth of tears beginning to gather behind his eyes, as if they were knocking on the door of his heart. It seemed that she saw them too.

"It's okay, honey, you can let it all out…I know you've been hurt, and I know you're angry and confused. So, go ahead and let it out. It does a soul good to let the waters run once in a while—the healing waters."

But while Mack could not stop the tears from filling his eyes, he was not ready to let go—not yet, not with this woman. With every effort he could muster, he kept himself from falling back into the black hole of his emotions. Meanwhile, this woman stood with her arms outstretched as if they were the very arms of his mother. He felt the presence of love. It was warm, inviting, melting.

"Not ready?" she responded. "That's okay, we'll do things on your terms and time."

24. Reflect on the defenses of Mack's heart and your heart. Does God enter those places? How? Reflect on "your terms and time."

MACK STEPPED BACK again, feeling a bit overwhelmed. "Are there more of you?" he asked a little hoarsely.

The three looked at one another and laughed.

Mack couldn't help but smile.

"No, Mackenzie." The black woman chuckled. "We is all that you get, and believe me, we're more than enough."

25. Consider the three whom Mack has met. How do his expectations compare with what he is experiencing?

"THEN," MACK STRUGGLED to ask, "which one of you is God?"

"I am," said all three in unison. Mack looked from one to the next, and even though he couldn't begin to grasp what he was seeing and hearing, he somehow believed them.

26. Reflections.

A PIECE OF Π

Honest Conversations with God

MACK TURNED AND faced him, shaking his head. "Am I going crazy? Am I supposed to believe that God is a big black woman with a questionable sense of humor?"

Jesus laughed. "She's a riot! You can always count on her to throw you a curve or two. She loves surprises, and even though you might not think it, her timing is always perfect."

1. Reflect on how God has shown up in your life. How could Mack believe God's timing is perfect in meeting God in the shack of his pain where his daughter was murdered?

"YOU'RE NOT *SUPPOSED* to do anything. You're free to do whatever you like." Jesus paused and then continued, trying to help by giving Mack a few suggestions. "I am working on a wood project in the shed. Sarayu is in the garden. Or you could go fishing, canoeing, or go in and talk to Papa."

"Well, I sort of feel obligated to go in and talk to him, uh, her."

"Oh"—now Jesus was serious—"don't go because you feel obligated. That won't get you any points around here. Go because it's what you *want* to do."

2. Reflect on the "should"s, "supposed to"s, and obligations in your life. Where do they come from? What does God have to do with them?

SUDDENLY MACK WANTED to ask a thousand questions, or say a thousand things, some of them unspeakable and terrible. He was sure that his face betrayed the emotions he was battling to control, and then in a flash of a second he shoved everything back into his battered heart's closet, locking the door on the way out. If she knew his inner conflict, she showed nothing by her expression—still open, full of life, and inviting.

3. Consider how our heart works and how God works in our heart. Let yourself be aware of the compartments and "battered closets" of your heart. You don't have to open them until you are ready, just be aware of them.

"NO SMALL ISSUE there," Mack interrupted with an awkward chuckle.

"Or maybe it's because of the failures of your *own* papa?"

Mack gasped involuntarily. He wasn't used to having deep secrets surface so quickly and openly. Instantly guilt and anger welled up and he wanted to lash out with a sarcastic remark in response. Mack felt as if he were dangling over a bottomless chasm and was afraid if he let any of it out, he would lose control of everything. He sought for safe footing but was only partially successful, finally answering through gritted teeth, "Maybe it's because I've never known *anyone* I could really call Papa."

4. Consider not only why it is so hard for Mack to call God "Papa," but also why it is so hard for him to open up his heart to God.

5. Reflect on how Papa is responding to Mack.

SHE DIDN'T HAVE to say it; he knew she understood what was going on inside him, and somehow he knew she cared about him more than anyone ever had. "If you let me, Mack, I'll be the papa you never had."

The offer was at once inviting and at the same time repulsive. He had always wanted a papa he could trust, but he wasn't sure he'd find it here, especially if this one couldn't even protect his Missy. A long silence hung between them. Mack was uncertain what to say, and she was in no hurry to let the moment pass easily.

"If you couldn't take care of Missy, how can I trust you to take care of me?" There, he'd said it—the question that had tormented him every day of *The Great Sadness*. Mack felt his face flush angry red as he stared at what he now considered to be some odd characterization of God, and he realized his hands were knotted into fists.

6. Reflections.

7. What are your thoughts and experiences with anger at God?

"MACK, I'M SO sorry." Tears began to trail down her cheeks. "I know what a great gulf this has put between us. I know you don't understand this yet, but I am especially fond of Missy, and you too."

8. Reflect on this passage and a God with tears in her eyes.

"HONEY, THERE'S NO easy answer that will take your pain away. Believe me, if I had one, I'd use it now. I have no magic wand to wave over you and make it all better. Life takes a bit of time and a lot of relationship."

9. Reflections.

"I'M NOT TRYING to make this harder for either of us. But *this* is a good place to start. I often find that getting head issues out of the way first makes the heart stuff easier to work on later...when you're ready."

She again picked up the wooden spoon, which was dripping with some sort of batter. "Mackenzie, I am neither male nor female, even though both genders are derived from my nature. If I choose to *appear* to you as a man or a woman, it's because I love you. For me to appear to you as a woman and suggest that you call me 'Papa' is simply to mix metaphors, to help you keep from falling so easily back into your religious conditioning."

She leaned forward as if to share a secret. "To reveal myself to you as a very large, white grandfather figure with flowing beard, like Gandalf, would simply reinforce your religious stereotypes, and this weekend is *not* about reinforcing your religious stereotypes."

10. Write down your thoughts about head issues, heart issues, and stereotypes (religious or others).

"OF COURSE I did." She was busy again, her back to him.

"Then was I free *not* to come? Did I not have a choice in the matter?"

Papa turned back to face him, now with flour and dough in her hands. "Good question—how deep would you like to go?" She didn't wait for a response, knowing that Mack didn't have one. Instead, she asked, "Do you believe you are free to leave?"

"I suppose I am. Am I?"

"Of course you are! I'm not interested in prisoners. You're free to walk out that door right now and go home to your empty house. Or you could go down to The Grind and hang out with Willie. Just because I know you're too curious to go, does that reduce your freedom to leave?"

She paused only briefly and then turned back to her task, talking to him over her shoulder. "Or, if you want to go just a wee bit deeper, we could talk about the nature of freedom itself. Does freedom mean that you are allowed to do whatever you want to do? Or we could talk about all the limiting influences in your life that actively work against your freedom. Your family genetic heritage, your specific DNA, your metabolic uniqueness, the quantum stuff that is going on at a subatomic level where only I am the always-present observer. Or the intrusion of your soul's sickness that inhibits and binds you, or the social influences around you, or the habits that have created synaptic bonds and pathways in your brain. And then there's advertising, propaganda, and paradigms. Inside that confluence of multifaceted inhibitors," she said, sighing, "what is freedom really?"

Mack just stood there, not knowing what to say.

"Only I can set you free, Mackenzie, but freedom can never be forced."

"I don't understand," replied Mack. "I don't even understand what you just told me."

She turned back and smiled. "I know. I didn't tell you so that you would understand right now. I told you for later. At this point, you don't even comprehend that freedom is an incremental process." Gently reaching out, she took Mack's hands in hers, flour-covered and all, and looking him straight in the eyes, she continued, "Mackenzie, the truth shall set you free and the truth has a name; he's over in the woodshop right now covered in sawdust. Everything is about *him*. And freedom is a process that happens inside a relationship with him. Then all that stuff you feel churnin' around *inside* will start to work its way out."

11. Don't just consider this one intellectually but explore the emotional aspects of your free will, particularly in the context of relationship.

"**How can you** really know how I feel?" Mack asked, looking back into her eyes.

Papa didn't answer, only looked down at their hands. His gaze followed hers and for the first time Mack noticed the scars on her wrists, like those he now assumed Jesus also had on his. She allowed him to tenderly touch the scars, outlines of a deep piercing, and he finally looked up again into her eyes. Tears were slowly making their way down her face, little pathways through the flour that dusted her cheeks.

"Don't ever think that what my Son chose to do didn't cost us dearly. Love always leaves a significant mark," she stated softly and gently. "We were there *together.*"

12. Reflect on a God who knows pain and loss.

"**You misunderstand the** mystery there. Regardless of what he *felt* at that moment, I never left him."

"How can you say that? You abandoned him just like you abandoned me!"

"Mackenzie, I never left him, and I have never left you."

"That makes no sense to me," he snapped.

"I know it doesn't, at least not yet. Will you at least consider this: when all you can see is your pain, perhaps then you lose sight of me?... Don't forget, the story didn't end in his sense of forsakenness. He found his way through it to put himself completely into my hands. Oh, what a moment that was!"

13. Reflections.

14. You may not be able to see God. You may not even believe in God right now. But will you at least consider this: "when all you can see is your pain, perhaps then you lose sight of God?"

"LIVING UNLOVED IS like clipping a bird's wings and removing its ability to fly. Not something I want for you."

There's the rub. He didn't *feel* particularly loved at the moment.

"Mack, pain has a way of clipping our wings and keeping us from being able to fly." She waited a moment, allowing her words to settle. "And if it's left unresolved for very long, you can almost forget that you were ever created to fly in the first place."

15. How and why do people tend to live unloved or at least fear rejection and abandonment?

"YES, BUT NOT exactly. At least not in the way you're thinking. Mackenzie, I am what some would say 'holy, and wholly other than you.' The problem is that many folks try to grasp some sense of who I am by taking the best version of themselves, projecting that to the nth degree, factoring in all the goodness they can perceive, which often isn't much, and then call *that* God. And while it may seem like a noble effort, the truth is that it falls pitifully short of who I really am. I'm not merely the best version of you that you can think of. I am far more than that, above and beyond all that you can ask or think."

16. Reflect on the difference between God and your projection of God.

"**ALTHOUGH BY NATURE** he is fully God, Jesus is fully human and lives as such. While never losing the innate ability to fly, he chooses moment by moment to remain grounded. That is why his name is Immanuel, 'God with us,' or 'God with *you*,' to be more precise."

"But what about all the miracles? The healings? Raising people from the dead? Doesn't that prove that Jesus was God—you know, more than human?"

"No, it proves that Jesus is truly human."

"What?"

"Mackenzie, *I* can fly, but humans can't. Jesus is fully human. Although he is also fully God, he has never drawn upon his nature as God to do anything. He has only lived out of his relationship with me, living in the very same manner that I desire to be in relationship with every human being. He is just the first to do it to the uttermost—the first to absolutely trust my life within him, the first to believe in my love and my goodness without regard for appearance or consequence."

17. **Who is Jesus, and what is his role? Atoning sacrifice? An example of other centered self-giving love? The one who is in the Father and the Father is in?**

18. **Reflect on Immanuel, "God with *you*."**

"**ONLY AS HE** rested in his relationship with me, and in our communion—our co-union—could he express my heart and will into any given circumstance. So, when you look at Jesus and it appears that he's flying, he really is...flying. But what you are actually seeing is me, my life in him. That's how he lives and acts as a true human, how every human is designed to live—out of my life.

"A bird's not defined by being grounded but by his ability to fly. Remember this, humans are defined not by their limitations, but by the intentions I have for them; not by what they seem to be, but by everything it means to be created in my image."

19. Reflect on living out of who we were created to be, not out of who we fear we are.

"BUT WHAT DIFFERENCE does it make that there are three of you, and you are all one God? Did I say that right?"

"Right enough." She grinned. "Mackenzie, it makes all the difference in the world!" She seemed to be enjoying this. "We are not three gods, and we are not talking about one god with three attitudes, like a man who is a husband, father, and worker. I am one God and I am three persons, and each of the three is fully and entirely the one.... What's important is this: if I were simply one God and only one Person, then you would find yourself in this creation without something wonderful, without something essential even. And I would be utterly other than I am."

"And we would be without...?" Mack didn't even know how to finish the question.

"Love and relationship. All love and relationship is possible for you *only* because it already exists within me, within God myself. Love is *not* the limitation; love is the flying. I *am* love."

20. Reflect on true loving relationship. If relationship is not already in God, where would we ever hope to find true relationship?

"YOU DO UNDERSTAND," she continued, "that unless I had an object to love—or, more accurately, a someone to love—if I did not have such a relationship within myself, then I would not be capable of love at all? You would have a god who could not love. Or maybe worse, you would have a god who, when he chose, could love only as a limitation of his nature. That kind of god could possibly act without love, and that would be a disaster. And that is surely *not* me."

With that, Papa stood up, went to the oven door, pulled out the freshly baked pie, set it on the counter, and, turning around as if to present herself, said, "The God who is—the I am who I am—cannot act apart from love!"

21. Reflect on "God cannot act apart from love."

"As much as you are able, rest in what trust you have in me, no matter how small, okay?"

22. Consider Mack's struggle for real trust in a real God in the middle of his real pain versus religious trust—an intellectual trust that most people, who grow up in church at least, are taught we are supposed to have.

He walked in and scanned the room. Could this even be the same place? He shuddered at the whisper of lurking dark thoughts and again locked them out. Across the room a hallway disappeared at an angle. Glancing around the corner into the living room, his eyes searched out the spot near the fireplace, but there was no stain marring the wood surface.

23. Look back at this paragraph near the beginning of this chapter. Paul Young has said that this was a mistake, that Missy's bloodstain should still be there. What do you think?

GOD ON THE DOCK

God in Relationship

IT MUST HAVE landed close to Papa because the lower portion of her skirt and bare feet were covered in the gooey mess. All three were laughing so hard that Mack didn't think they were breathing. Sarayu said something about humans being clumsy, and all three started roaring again. Finally, Jesus brushed past Mack and returned a minute later with a large basin of water and towels. Sarayu had already started wiping the goop from the floor and cupboards, but Jesus went straight to Papa and, kneeling at her feet, began to wipe off the front of her clothes. He worked down to her feet and gently lifted one foot at a time, which he directed into the basin where he cleaned and massaged it.

"Ooooh, that feels soooo good!" exclaimed Papa as she continued her tasks at the counter.

As he leaned against the doorway watching, Mack's mind was full of thoughts. So this was God in relationship?

1. Reflect on relationships. What are some of the different things that relationships in your life are based upon? What does this relationship appear to be based upon?

"REMEMBER THAT CHOOSING to stay on the ground is a choice to facilitate a relationship, to honor it. Mackenzie, you do this yourself. You don't play a game or color a picture with a child to show your superiority. Rather, you choose to limit yourself so as to facilitate and honor that relationship. You will even lose a competition to accomplish love. It is not about winning and losing, but about love and respect."

"So when I am telling you about my children...?"

"We have limited ourselves out of respect for you. We are not bringing to mind, as it were, our knowledge of your children. As we are listening to you, it is as if this is the first time we have known about them, and we take great delight in seeing them through your eyes."

2. Reflect on this conversation and God's delight.

"RELATIONSHIPS ARE NEVER about power, and one way to avoid the will to hold power over another is to choose to limit oneself—to serve. Humans often do this—in touching the infirm and sick, in serving the ones whose minds have left to wander, in relating to the poor, in loving the very old and the very young, or even in caring for the other who has assumed a position of power over them."

3. Reflect on relationships, power, and serving others.

MACK HAD TO suppress a snicker at the thought of God having devotions. Images of family devotions from his childhood came spilling into his mind, not exactly good memories. Often, it was a tedious and boring exercise in coming up with the right answers, or, rather, the same old answers to the same old Bible story questions, and then trying to stay awake during his father's excruciatingly long prayers....

Instead, Jesus reached across the table and took Papa's hands in his, scars now clearly visible on his wrists. Mack sat transfixed as he watched Jesus kiss his Father's hands and then look deep into his Father's eyes and finally say, "Papa, I loved watching you today as you made yourself fully available to take Mack's pain into yourself and then gave him space to choose his own timing. You honored him, and you honored me. To listen to you whisper love and calm into his heart was truly incredible. What a joy to watch! I love being your Son."

…What was he witnessing? Something simple, warm, intimate, genuine; this was holy. Holiness had always been a cold and sterile concept to Mack, but *this* was neither.

4. Consider the contrast between Mack's family devotions as a child and what he was experiencing.

5. How would you define *holy* and the holiness of God?

"WHAT ABOUT THE others?" Mack asked.

"I'm here," replied Jesus. "I'm always here."

Mack nodded. This presence-of-God thing, although hard to grasp, seemed to be steadily penetrating past his mind and into his heart. He let it go at that.

6. Reflect on "this presence-of-God thing."

"C'MON," SAID JESUS, interrupting Mack's thoughts. "I know you enjoy looking at stars! Want to?" He sounded just like a child full of anticipation and expectancy....

"Wow!" he whispered.

"Incredible!" whispered Jesus, his head near Mack's in the darkness. "I never get tired of this."

...Mack was not sure how to describe what he felt, but as they continued to lie in silence, gazing into the celestial display, watching and listening, he knew in his heart that this too was holy.

7. **Reflect on moments with this Jesus. Have you ever experienced this kind of holy?**

"I AM THE best way any human can relate to Papa or Sarayu. To see me is to see them. The love you sense from me is no different from how they love you. And believe me, Papa and Sarayu are just as real as I am, though, as you've seen in far different ways."

"Speaking of Sarayu, is she the Holy Spirit?"

"Yes. She is creativity; she is action; she is the breathing of life; she is much more. She is *my* Spirit...."

"Elousia," the voice said reverently from the dark next to him. "That is a wonderful name. *El* is my name as Creator God, but *ousia* is 'being' or 'that which is truly real,' so the name means 'the Creator God who is truly real and the ground of all being.' Now that is also a beautiful name."

8. **Reflect on Papa, Jesus, and Sarayu.**

"SO THEN, WHERE does that leave us?" He felt as if he were asking the question for the entire human race.

"Right where you were always intended to be. In the very center of our love and our purpose."

Again a pause, then, "I suppose I can live with that."

9. So where does that leave us?

THE WORDS, THOUGH delivered kindly, stung. Stung what, exactly? Mack lay there a few seconds and realized that as much as he thought he knew Jesus, perhaps he didn't...not really. Maybe what he knew was an icon, an ideal, an image through which he tried to grasp a sense of spirituality, but not a real person. "Why is that?" he finally asked. "You said if I really knew you it wouldn't matter what you looked like."

10. Reflect on knowing someone. What is the difference between knowing about someone and knowing someone?

11. How much do we develop a relationship with our image of someone versus relating to the reality of someone?

12. Do we tend to do this even more with God? Why?

"**IT IS QUITE** simple really. *Being* always transcends appearance—that which only seems to be. Once you begin to know the being behind the very pretty or very ugly face, as determined by your bias, the surface appearances fade away until they simply no longer matter. That is why Elousia is such a wonderful name. God, who is the ground of all being, dwells in, around, and through all things—ultimately emerging as the real—and any appearances that mask that reality will fall away."

13. Reflections.

"**YOU SAID** I don't really know you. It would be a lot easier if we could always talk like this."

"Admittedly, Mack, this is special. You were really stuck and we wanted to help you crawl out of your pain. But don't think that just because I'm not visible, our relationship has to be less real. It will be different, but perhaps even more real."

14. Consider the physical versus the spiritual world and Mack's question. Reflect on what is "real."

"**MY PURPOSE FROM** the beginning was to live in you and you in me."

"Wait, wait. Wait a minute. How can that happen? If you're still fully human, how can you be inside me?"

"Astounding, isn't it? It's Papa's miracle. It is the power of Sarayu, my Spirit, the Spirit of God who restores the union that was lost so long ago. Me? I choose to live moment by moment fully human. I am fully God, but I am human to the core. Like I said, it's Papa's miracle."

Mack was lying in the darkness, listening intently. "Aren't you talking about a real indwelling, not just some positional, theological thing?"

"Of course," answered Jesus, his voice strong and sure. "It's what everything is all about. The human, formed out of the physical material creation, can once more be fully indwelt by spiritual life, my life. It requires that a very real dynamic and active union exists."

"I'm praying not only for them but also for those who will believe in me because of them and their witness about me. The goal is for all of them to become one heart and mind—just as you, Father, are in me and I in you, so they might be one heart and mind with us. Then the world might believe that you, in fact, sent me. The same glory you gave me, I gave them, so they'll be as unified and together as we are—I in them and you in me. Then they'll be mature in this oneness, and give the godless world evidence that you've sent me and loved them in the same way you've loved me. Father, I want those you gave me to be with me, right where I am, so they can see my glory, the splendor you gave me, having loved me long before there ever was a world. Righteous Father, the world has never known you, but I have known you, and these disciples know that you sent me on this mission. I have made your very being known to them—who you are and what you do— and continue to make it known, so that your love for me might be in them exactly as I am in them."

JOHN 17:20–26 MSG

15. Reflections.

"SOMETIMES YOU SOUND so...I mean, here I am, lying next to God Almighty, and you really sound so..."

"Human?" Jesus offered. "But ugly." And with that he began to chuckle, quietly and restrained at first, but after a couple of snorts, laughter simply started tumbling out. It was infectious, and Mack found himself swept along from somewhere deep inside. He had not laughed from down there in a long time. Jesus reached over and hugged him, shaking from his own spasms of mirth, and Mack felt more clean and alive and well than he had since...well, he couldn't remember when.

16. **Reflect on how the heart heals. Give yourself time to lie beside Jesus and look at the stars, to feel his hug, to feel his delight.**

MACK LAY THERE realizing that he was now feeling guilty about enjoying himself, about laughing, and even in the darkness he could feel *The Great Sadness* roll in and over him.

"Jesus?" he whispered as his voice choked. "I feel so lost."

A hand reached out and squeezed his and didn't let go. "I know, Mack. But it's not true. I am with you and I'm not lost. I'm sorry it feels that way, but hear me clearly: *you are not lost.*"

17. **Reflect on how we try to heal our heart on our own versus in relationship.**

A Breakfast of Champions

The Mud, Dark Holes, and the Things That Keep You from Soaring

SNUGGLING LIKE A small child deep inside the heavy down comforter, he had made it through only a couple of verses before the Bible somehow left his hand, the light somehow turned off, someone kissed him on the cheek, and he was lifting gently off the ground in a flying dream.

1. What would it be like to be tucked in by God every night?

AS HE SOARED at will over rugged mountains and crystal white seashores, reveling in the missed wonder of dream flight, suddenly something grabbed him by the ankle and tore him out of the sky. In a matter of seconds he was dragged from the heights and violently thrown face-first onto a muddy and deeply rutted road. Thunder shook the ground and rain instantly drenched him to the bone. And there it came again, lightning illuminating the face of his daughter as she soundlessly screamed "Daddy" and then turned to run into the darkness, her red dress visible only for a few brief flashes and then gone. He fought with all his strength to extricate himself from the mud and the water, only succeeding in being sucked deeper into its grasp. And just as he was being taken under he woke with a gasp.

2. Does *The Great Sadness* ground Mack from soaring in more ways than just dream flight?

3. What tries to pull you down at times?

HE LET OUT a deep, heavy sigh. And if God was really here, why hadn't he taken his nightmares away?

4. Does God's presence take away all our nightmares? Why or why not?

THE THREE CANOES resting easily at intervals along the dock looked inviting, but Mack shrugged off the thought. Canoes were no longer a joy. Too many bad memories.

5. Reflect on bad memories and nightmares. How does body, mind, and spirit process "bad things"?

"SO, HONEY," PAPA asked, continuing busily with whatever she was doing, "how were your dreams last night? Dreams are sometimes important, you know. They can be a way of openin' up the window and lettin' the bad air out."

Mack knew this was an invitation to unlock the door to his terrors, but at the moment he wasn't ready to invite her into that hole with him. "I slept fine, thank you," he responded and then quickly changed the subject.

6. Why is it hard for Mack to invite God or anyone "into that hole with him"?

A BREAKFAST OF CHAMPIONS   63

7. Do you see yourself and others struggle with this as well?

"IS HE YOUR favorite? Bruce, I mean?"

She stopped and looked at him. "Mackenzie, I have no favorites. I am just especially fond of him."

"You seem to be especially fond of a lot of people," Mack observed with a suspicious look. "Are there any you are *not* especially fond of?"

8. Does God have "favorites"? Do we want God to have "favorites" sometimes?

"ARE THERE ANY you are *not* especially fond of?"

She lifted her head and rolled her eyes as if she were mentally going through the catalog of every being ever created. "Nope, I haven't been able to find any. Guess that's jes' the way I is."

Mack was interested. "Do you ever get mad at any of them?"

"Sho 'nuff! What parent doesn't? There is a lot to be mad about in the mess my kids have made and in the mess they're in. I don't like a lot of the choices they make, but that anger—especially for me—is an expression of love all the same. I love the ones I am angry with just as much as those I'm not."

"But—" Mack paused. "What about your wrath? It seems to me that if you're going to pretend to be God Almighty, you need to be a lot angrier."

9. Reflect on God's anger. How can anger be an expression of love?

10. When is anger clearly not an expression of love?

11. Is God's anger ever not an expression of love?

12. Is man's anger ever not an expression of love?

"**BUT IF YOU** are God, aren't you the One spilling out great bowls of wrath and throwing people into a burning lake of fire?" Mack could feel his deep anger emerging again, pushing out the questions in front of it, and he was a little chagrined at his own lack of self-control. But he asked anyway, "Honestly, don't you enjoy punishing those who disappoint you?"

At that, Papa stopped her preparations and turned toward Mack. He could see a deep sadness in her eyes. "I am not who you think I am, Mackenzie. I don't need to punish people for sin. Sin is its own punishment, devouring you from the inside. It's not my purpose to punish it; it's my joy to cure it."

13. Consider God's perspective on sin. Then reflect on how your ideas about God and sin have developed over time.

THEN TURNING BACK to Jesus he added, "I love the way you treat each other. It's certainly not how I expected God to be."

"How do you mean?"

"Well, I know that you are one and all, and that there are three of you. But you respond with such graciousness to each other. Isn't one of you more the boss than the other two?"

The three looked at one another as if they had never thought of such a question.

"I mean," Mack hurried on, "I have always thought of God the Father as sort of being the boss and Jesus as the one following orders, you know, being obedient. I'm not sure how the Holy Spirit fits in exactly. He...I mean, she...

uh..." Mack tried not to look at Sarayu as he stumbled for words. "Whatever—the Spirit always seemed kind of a...uh..."

"A free Spirit?" offered Papa.

"Exactly—a free spirit, but still under the direction of the Father. Does that make sense?"

14. **Consider Mack's struggle. In your opinion, how does the Father, Son, and Spirit relate to one another? Could it be that the very heart and nature of God is relational? (This one and the next several questions are an opportunity for deep intellectual consideration but also deep emotional reflection.)**

"MACKENZIE, WE HAVE no concept of final authority among us, only unity. We are in a *circle* of relationship, not a chain of command or 'great chain of being,' as your ancestors termed it. What you're seeing here is relationship without any overlay of power. We don't need power over the other because we are always looking out for the best. Hierarchy would make no sense among us. Actually, this is your problem, not ours."

"Really? How so?"

"Humans are so lost and damaged that to you it is almost incomprehensible that people could work or live together without someone being in charge."

15. **Reflect on unity, final authority, power, and the unique self.**

"IT'S ONE REASON why experiencing true relationship is so difficult for you," Jesus added. "Once you have a hierarchy you need rules to protect and administer it, and then you need law and the enforcement of the rules, and you end up with some kind of chain of command or a system of order that destroys relationship rather than promotes it. You rarely see or experience relationship apart from power. Hierarchy imposes laws and rules and you end up missing the wonder of relationship that we intended for you."

...Sarayu continued, "When you chose independence over relationship, you became a danger to one another. Others became objects to be manipulated or managed for your own happiness. Authority, as you usually think of it, is merely the excuse the strong ones use to make others conform to what they want."

"Isn't it helpful in keeping people from fighting endlessly or getting hurt?"

"Sometimes. But in a selfish world it is also used to inflict great harm."

"But don't you use it to restrain evil?"

"We carefully respect your choices, so we work within your systems even while we seek to free you from them."

16. Reflect on hierarchy and relationship.

JESUS PICKED UP the conversation. "As the crowning glory of creation, you were made in our image, unencumbered by structure and free to simply 'be' in relationship with me and one another. If you had truly learned to regard one another's concerns as significant as your own, there would be no need for hierarchy."

17. Reflect on the freedom to "be."

18. Reflect on how we use structure and systems to manage relationships rather than mutual respect and other centered self-giving love.

"BUT HOW COULD we ever change that? People will just use us."

"They most likely will. But we're not asking you to do it with others, Mack. We're asking you to do it with us. That's the only place it can begin. We won't use you."

"Mack," said Papa with an intensity that caused him to listen very carefully, "we want to share with you the love and joy and freedom and light that we already know within ourselves. We created you, the human, to be in face-to-face relationship with us, to join our circle of love. As difficult as it will be for you to understand, everything that has taken place is occurring exactly according to this purpose, without violating choice or will."

"How can you say that with all the pain in this world, all the wars and disasters that destroy thousands?" Mack's voice quieted to a whisper. "And what is the value in a little girl being murdered by some twisted deviant?" There it was again, the question that lay burning a hole in his soul. "You may not cause those things, but you certainly don't stop them."

19. **Reflections. As you write, give voice to the various emotional states you felt as you read this passage. (For a more in-depth experience, now and through the rest of your journey through *The Shack*, take time to write out separately a unique voice for each emotional state you become aware of as you read. For example, write out all the angry thoughts when you feel angry, but if you also feel guilt, hurt, or love, on separate pages write out thoughts from each of those emotional states. Don't allow one emotional state to dominate, but allow yourself to reflect on the complexity of your internal world.)**

20. **Reflect on loving others and loving God in a fallen world where bad things happen.**

"MACKENZIE," PAPA ANSWERED tenderly, seemingly not offended in the least by his accusation, "there are millions of reasons to allow pain and hurt and suffering rather than to eradicate them, but most of those reasons can be understood only within each person's story. I am not evil. You are the ones who embrace fear and pain and power and rights so readily in your relationships.

But your choices are also not stronger than my purposes, and I will use every choice you make for the ultimate good and the most loving outcome."

21. Why does God allow pain and suffering?

"YOU SEE PAIN and death as ultimate evils and God as the ultimate betrayer, or perhaps, at best, as fundamentally untrustworthy. You dictate the terms and judge my actions and find me guilty.

"The real underlying flaw in your life, Mackenzie, is that you don't think I am good."

22. Reflect on this statement as it applies to Mack, others, and you.

SARAYU SPOKE. "MACKENZIE, you cannot produce trust just as you cannot 'do' humility. It either is or is not. Trust is the fruit of a relationship in which you know you are loved. Because you do not know that I love you, you cannot trust me."

Again there was silence, and finally Mack looked up at Papa and spoke. "I don't know how to change that."

"You can't, not alone. But together we will watch that change take place. For now I just want you to be with me and discover that our relationship is not about performance or your having to please me. I'm not a bully, not some self-centered demanding little deity insisting on my own way. I am good, and I desire only what is best for you. You cannot find that through guilt or condemnation or coercion, only through a relationship of love. And I do love you."

23. Reflect on trust and a loving relationship versus guilt, condemnation, and coercion.

A LONG TIME AGO,
IN A GARDEN FAR, FAR AWAY

The Garden of Creation in Your Heart

1. How would you describe the Holy Spirit?

2. As you read this chapter, reflect on the garden Mack and Sarayu enter.

MACK LEANED ON his rake and looked around the garden and then at the red welts on his arms. "Sarayu, I know you are the Creator, but did you make the poisonous plants, stinging nettles, and mosquitoes too?"

"Mackenzie," responded Sarayu, seeming to move in tandem with the breezes, "a created being can only take what already exists and from it fashion something different."

"So, you are saying that you…"

"…created everything that actually exists, including what you consider the bad stuff," Sarayu completed his sentence. "But when I created it, it was only good, because that is just the way I am." She seemed to almost billow into a curtsy before resuming her task.

"But," Mack continued, not satisfied, "then why has so much of the 'good' gone 'bad'?"

Now Sarayu paused before answering. "You humans, so little in your own eyes. You are truly blind to your own place in the creation. Having chosen the ravaged path of independence, you don't even comprehend that you are dragging the entire creation along with you."

3. Reflect on "creator and created," "good and bad," and the fall of creation discussed in this passage. Let yourself be aware of your emotions and the different ways those emotional places inside respond to these issues.

SARAYU LAUGHED. "I am here, Mack. There are times when it is safe to touch, and times when precautions must be taken. That is the wonder and adventure of exploration, a piece of what you call science—to discern and discover what we have hidden for you to find."

"So why did you hide it?" Mack inquired.

"Why do children love to hide and seek? Ask any person who has a passion to explore and discover and create. The choice to hide so many wonders from you is an act of love that is a gift inside the process of life."

4. Reflect on this passage and your passion to explore, discover, and create.

MACK GINGERLY REACHED out and took the poisonous twig. "If you had not told me this was safe to touch, would it have poisoned me?"

"Of course! But if I direct you to touch, that is different. For any created being, autonomy is lunacy. Freedom involves trust and obedience inside a relationship of love. So, if you are not hearing my voice, it would be wise to take the time to understand the nature of the plant."

5. Reflect on "freedom and safety" in our independence versus inside a relationship of love.

"SO WHY CREATE poisonous plants at all?" Mack queried, handing back the twig.

"Your question presumes that poison is bad, that such creations have no purpose. Many of these so-called bad plants, like this one, contain incredible properties for healing or are necessary for some of the most magnificent wonders when combined with something else. Humans have a great capacity for declaring something good or evil, without truly knowing."

6. Reflect on this passage and humans "great capacity for declaring something good or evil without truly knowing."

"WHEN SOMETHING HAPPENS to you, how do you determine whether it is good or evil?"

Mack thought for a moment before answering. "Well, I haven't really thought about that. I guess I would say that something is good when I like it—when it makes me feel good or gives me a sense of security. Conversely, I'd call something evil that causes me pain or costs me something I want."

"So it is pretty subjective then?"

"I guess it is."

"And how confident are you in your ability to discern what indeed is good for you, or what is evil?"

"To be honest," said Mack, "I tend to sound justifiably angry when somebody is threatening my 'good,' you know, what I think I deserve. But I'm not really sure I have any logical ground for deciding what is actually good or evil, except how something or someone affects me."

7. **How do you determine whether something is good or evil? (Listen to your emotions. Reflect on the things in your life that trigger strong mixed emotional states. As you continue on this journey, give each emotion a voice like characters in a story or crew members on a ship. Your logical problem solver or intellect is a crew member as well. You may recognize one or two crew members that try to dominate. Allow yourself to hear from and feel each one as openly and honestly as you can.)**

SARAYU INTERRUPTED. "THEN it is you who determines good and evil. You become the judge. And to make things more confusing, that which you determine to be good will change over time and circumstance. And then, beyond that and even worse, there are billions of you, each determining what is good and what is evil. So when your good and evil clashes with your neighbor's, fights and arguments ensue and even wars break out.... And if there is no reality of good that is absolute, then you have lost any basis for judging. It is just language, and one might as well exchange the word *good* for the word *evil.*"

8. **Reflect on this passage. On what basis do your emotional crew members determine good and evil? On what basis does your intellectual/ logical crew member determine good and evil? (Allow yourself to be aware of the many different levels of processing that go on inside. Reflect on each emotional state or crew member and the automatic thoughts that go with them. Reflect on the processing of mixed emotional states. Think of it as conversations between crew members. Now reflect on how these inner conversations get resolved. What standards of right and wrong or core beliefs are used to govern these inner conversations? Be careful here not to just think your way through this**

journey. Feel the inner conversations, emotions, and conflicts. As we discussed in the last chapter, giving voice to each emotional state or crew member in separate journal entries sometimes helps.)

"**Indeed! The choice** to eat of that tree tore the universe apart, divorcing the spiritual from the physical. They died, expelling in the breath of their choice the very breath of God."

9. Read about "The Fall" in Genesis 3 and reflect on this passage.

"**I can see** now," confessed Mack, "that I spend most of my time and energy trying to acquire what I have determined to be good, whether it's financial security or health or retirement or whatever. And I spend a huge amount of energy and worry fearing what I've determined to be evil." Mack sighed deeply.

"Such truth in that," said Sarayu gently. "Remember this. It allows you to play God in your independence. That's why a part of you prefers not to see me. And you don't need me at all to create your list of good and evil. But you do need me if you have any desire to stop such an insane lust for independence.... You must give up your right to decide what is good and evil on your own terms. That is a hard pill to swallow—choosing to live only in me. To do that, you must know me enough to trust me and learn to rest in my inherent goodness."

10. How does your assessment of good and evil affect the way you spend your time and energy? And how does trust in God's goodness impact that? (It is okay if you are not sure about God and His goodness. Reflect on that as well.)

SARAYU TURNED TOWARD Mack; at least that was his impression. "Mackenzie, *evil* is a word we use to describe the absence of good, just as we use the word *darkness* to describe the absence of light or *death* to describe the absence of life. Both evil and darkness can only be understood in relation to light and good; they do not have any actual existence. I am light and I am good. I am love and there is no darkness in me. Light and Good actually exist. So, removing yourself from me will plunge you into darkness. Declaring independence will result in evil because apart from me, you can draw only upon yourself. That is death because you have separated yourself from me: Life."

11. **This might be seen as a controversial statement by some. Reflect on the existence of good and evil, light and dark, life and death.**

"WOW!" MACK EXCLAIMED, sitting back for a moment. "That really helps. But I can also see that giving up my independent right is not going to be an easy process. It could mean that—"

Sarayu interrupted his sentence again. "That in one instance, the good may be the presence of cancer or the loss of income—or even a life."

"Yeah, but tell that to the person with cancer or the father whose daughter is dead," Mack said, a little more sarcastically than he had intended.

"Oh, Mackenzie," reassured Sarayu. "Don't you think we have them in mind as well? Each of them was the center of another story that is untold."

"But—" Mack could feel his control getting away as he drove his shovel in hard—"Didn't Missy have a right to be protected?"

"No, Mack. A child is protected because she is loved, not because she has a right to be protected."

12. **Now the theology of good and evil is getting personal for Mack. Reflect on how it gets personal for you.**

13. **What is meant by the statement, "Each of them is in the center of another story that is untold"?**

"RIGHTS ARE WHERE survivors go, so that they won't have to work out relationships."

14. **Reflections.**

"MACKENZIE, JESUS DIDN'T hold on to any rights. He willingly became a servant and lives out of his relationship to Papa. He gave up everything, so that by his dependent life he opened a door that would allow you to live free enough to give up your rights."

15. **Reflect on living out of a loving, dependent relationship that is freeing versus living out of a demand for rights, independence, and controlling structure that we may call relationship.**

"I DIDN'T DO that much, really," he said apologetically. "I mean, look at this mess." His gaze moved over the garden that surrounded them. "But it really is beautiful, and full of you, Sarayu. Even though it seems like lots of work still needs to be done, I feel strangely at home and comfortable here."

The two looked at each other and grinned.

Sarayu stepped toward him until she had invaded his personal space. "And well you should, Mackenzie, because this garden is your soul. This mess is *you*! Together, you and I, we have been working with a purpose in your heart. And it is wild and beautiful and perfectly in process. To you it seems like a mess, but I see a perfect pattern emerging and growing and alive—a living fractal."

16. Reflect on Mack's garden and your own. If you have time, do something artistic to represent and reflect on the garden of your soul.

THE IMPACT OF her words almost crumbled all of Mack's reserve. He looked again at their garden—his garden—and it really was a mess, but incredible and wonderful at the same time. And beyond that, Papa was here and Sarayu loved the mess. It was almost too much to comprehend, and once again his carefully guarded emotions threatened to spill over.

17. Reflect on the Father, Son, and Holy Spirit in the mess of your soul.

18. Are there walls you have built to hide parts of your heart and soul? How is that working out for you?

WADE IN THE WATER

The Present on or in the Water

1. What stood out to you the most in the last chapter?

2. What was most challenging about the last chapter?

WHAT JESUS HAD been suggesting, Mack finally allowed into his consciousness. He was talking about walking on the water. Jesus, anticipating his hesitation, asserted, "C'mon, Mack. If Peter can do it..."

Mack laughed, more out of nerves than anything. To be sure, he asked one more time, "You want me to walk *on* the water...?"

3. What has God invited you to do lately that has caused you to question, "You want me to...?"

"TELL ME WHAT you are afraid of, Mack."

4. What are you afraid of?

"WELL, LET ME see. What am I afraid of?" began Mack. "Well, I am afraid of looking like an idiot. I am afraid that you are making fun of me and that I will sink like a rock. I imagine that—"

"Exactly," Jesus interrupted. "You imagine. Such a powerful ability, the imagination! That power alone makes you so like us. But without wisdom, imagination is a cruel taskmaster."

5. Reflect on imagination with and without wisdom.

"IF I MAY prove my case, do you think humans were designed to live in the present or the past or the future?"

6. How would you answer this question?

"BUT NOW TELL me, where do *you* spend most of your time in your mind, in your imagination: in the present, in the past, or in the future?"

7. How would you answer that?

"NOT UNLIKE MOST people. When I dwell with you, I do so in the present—I live in the present. Not the past, although much can be remembered and learned by looking back, but only for a visit, not an extended stay. And for sure, I do not dwell in the future you visualize or imagine. Mack, do you realize that your imagination of the future, which is almost always dictated by fear of some kind, rarely, if ever, pictures me there with you?... It is your desperate attempt to get some control over something you can't. It is impossible for you to take power over the future because it isn't even real, nor will it ever be real. You try and play God, imagining the evil that you fear becoming reality, and then you try and make plans and contingencies to avoid what you fear."

8. Reflections.

"SO WHY DO I have so much fear in my life?"

"Because you don't believe. You don't know that we love you. The person who lives by his fears will not find freedom in my love. I am not talking about rational fears regarding legitimate dangers, but imagined fears, and especially the projection of those into the future. To the degree that those fears have a place in your life, you neither believe I am good nor know deep in your heart that I love you. You sing about it, you talk about it, but you don't know it."

9. So why do you have fears in your life?

WALKING ON THE water with Jesus seemed like the most natural way to cross a lake, and Mack was grinning ear to ear just thinking about what he was doing. He would occasionally look down to see if he could see any lake trout.

"This is utterly ridiculous and impossible, you know!" he finally exclaimed.

10. Is God loving, compassionate, and present with you but impotent, or have you walked on water with Jesus lately?

ONLY THEN DID he look up and across the lake. The beauty was staggering. He could make out the shack, where smoke leisurely rose from the red-brick chimney as it nestled against the greens of the orchard and forest. But dwarfing it all was a massive range of mountains that hovered above and behind, like sentinels standing guard. Mack simply sat, Jesus next to him, and inhaled the visual symphony.

11. What do you see when you survey the landscape of your pain? (Remember what the shack is for Mack.) Why?

12. Does God exist there? If so, what kind of God?

"So why don't you fix it?" Mack asked, munching on his sandwich. "The earth, I mean."

13. Reflect on the problem of pain and decay in the world.

"Because we gave it to you."

"Can't you take it back?"

"Of course we could, but then the story would end before it was consummated."

Mack gave Jesus a blank look.

"Have you noticed that even though you call me 'Lord' and 'King,' I have never really acted in that capacity with you? I've never taken control of your choices or forced you to do anything, even when what you were about to do was destructive or hurtful to yourself and others."

Mack looked back at the lake before responding. "I would have preferred that you did take control at times. It would have saved me and people I care about a lot of pain."

14. Reflect on the problem of "free will."

"That's the beauty you see in my relationship with Abba and Sarayu. We are indeed submitted to one another and have always been so and always will be. Papa is as much submitted to me as I to him, or Sarayu to me, or Papa to her. Submission is not about authority and it is not obedience; it is all about relationships of love and respect. In fact, we are submitted to you in the same way."

Mack was surprised. "How can that be? Why would the God of the universe want to be submitted to me?"

"Because we want you to join us in our circle of relationship. I don't want slaves to my will; I want brothers and sisters who will share life with me."

15. Reflect on submission, authority, obedience, respect, and love in relationships.

"AND ALL I wanted was a God who will just fix everything so no one gets hurt."

16. What kind of God do you find yourself wanting sometimes?

"YOU'RE NOT JUST dealing with Missy's murder. There's a larger twisting that makes sharing life with us difficult. The world is broken because in Eden you abandoned relationship with us to assert your own independence. Most men have expressed it by turning to the work of their hands and the sweat of their brows to find their identity, value, and security. By choosing to declare what's good and evil you seek to determine your own destiny. It was this turning that has caused so much pain."

17. Reflect on identity, value, and security.

18. How do those things develop in independence from God versus in relationship with God?

"BUT THAT ISN'T all. The woman's desire—and the word is actually her *turn-ing*—so the woman's turning was not to the works of her hands but to the man, and his response was to rule 'over' her, to take power over her, to become the ruler. Before the choosing, she found her identity, her security, and her understanding of good and evil only in me, as did man.... Women in general will find it difficult to turn from a man and stop demanding that he meet their needs, provide security, and protect their identity, and return to me. Men in general find it very hard to turn from the works of their hands, their own quests for power and security and significance, and return to me."

19. Reflect on what you turn to for identity, security, and significance.

"MACK, DON'T YOU see how filling roles is the opposite of relationship? We want male and female to be counterparts, face-to-face equals, each unique and different, distinctive in gender but complementary, and each empowered uniquely by Sarayu, from whom all true power and authority originate. Remember, I am not about performance and fitting into man-made structures; I am about being."

20. Reflect on how and why we try to find identity in roles versus "being."

"WE DIDN'T CREATE man to live alone; she was purposed from the beginning. By taking her out of him, he birthed her in a sense. We created a circle of relationship, like our own, but for humans. She, out *of* him, and now all the males, including me, birthed through her, and all originating, or birthed, from God."

"Oh, I get it," Mack said, stopping in mid-throw. "If the female had been created first, there would have been no circle of relationship, and thus no possibility of a fully equal face-to-face relationship between the male and the female. Right?"

"Exactly right, Mack." Jesus looked at him and grinned. "Our desire was to create a being that had a fully equal and powerful counterpart, the male and the female. But your independence with its quest for power and fulfillment actually destroys the relationship your heart longs for."

21. Reflect on God's design for male and female and relationship in general.

"MACK, JUST LIKE love, submission is not something that you can do, especially not on your own. Apart from my life inside you, you can't submit to Nan, or your children, or anyone else in your life, including Papa."

"You mean," Mack interjected a little sarcastically, "that I can't just ask, 'What would Jesus do?'"

Jesus chuckled. "Good intentions; bad idea. Let me know how it works for you, if that's the way you choose to go." He paused and grew sober. "Seriously, my life was not meant to be an example to copy. Being my follower is not trying to 'be like Jesus,' it means your independence is killed. I came to give you life, real life, my life. We will come and live our life inside you, so that you begin to see with our eyes, and hear with our ears, and touch with our hands, and think like we do. But we will never force that union on you."

22. Reflect on trying to "be like Jesus" versus being in relationship with Jesus.

HERE COME DA JUDGE

Judging and Being Judged, Knowing and Being Known

1. Consider what it must have been like for Mack to walk away from Jesus and step into that dark tunnel.

SHE IS BEAUTY, he thought. *Everything that sensuality strives to be, but falls painfully short....*

That was all it took for Mack to understand that he was expected and welcomed here. She looked strangely familiar, as if he might have known or glimpsed her somewhere in the past, only he knew that he had never truly seen or met her before.

2. Reflect on Mack's thought.

3. Have you ever considered that one day you may meet face-to-face with beings that we now only understand as concepts? What would it be like for you to sit down and have a conversation with Beauty, Wisdom, Justice, Faith, or...Love? Who would you most like to talk to, and who would you be afraid to face?

"IN SOME SENSE every parent does love their children," she responded, ignoring his second question. "But some parents are too broken to love them well and others are barely able to love them at all; you should understand that. But you, you do love your children well—very well."

4. **Reflections. (You may understand parents who are too broken to love well. Consider a letter to or some reflections on your parents. Let wisdom be your guide. There is no pressure toward reconciliation here, just reflection. Rarely would I recommend sending the letter at this stage of your journey unless clearly prompted by Sarayu.)**

"SO THEN, MACKENZIE, may I ask which of your children you love the most?"

Mack smiled inside. As the kids had come along, he had wrestled to answer this very question. "I don't love any one of them more than any of the others. I love each of them differently..."

"Explain that to me, Mackenzie," she said with interest.

"Well, each one of my children is unique. And that uniqueness and special personhood calls out a unique response from me." Mack settled back into his chair. "I remember after Jon, my first, was born. I was so captivated by the wonder of who this little life was that I actually worried about whether I would have anything left to love a second child with. But when Tyler came along, it was as if he brought with him a special gift for me, a whole new capacity to love him specially. Come to think of it, it's like when Papa says she is especially fond of someone. When I think of each of my children individually, I find that I am especially fond of each one."

5. **Reflect on the kind of love they are discussing. What has been your experience with receiving and expressing that kind of love?**

6. Reflect on our capacity to love.

"BUT WHAT ABOUT when they do not behave, or they make choices other than those you would want them to make, or they are just belligerent and rude? What about when they embarrass you in front of others? How does that affect your love for them?"

Mack responded slowly and deliberately. "It doesn't, really." He knew that what he was saying was true, even if Katie didn't believe it sometimes. "I admit that it does affect me and sometimes I get embarrassed or angry, but even when they act badly, they are still my sons and my daughter, they are still Josh and Kate, and they will be forever. What they do might affect my pride, but not my love for them."

7. How does the behavior of someone you love affect you?

8. What about someone you don't love?

9. What is the difference?

"YOU ARE WISE in the ways of real love, Mackenzie. So many believe that it is love that grows, but it is the *knowing* that grows and love simply expands to contain it. Love is just the skin of knowing. Mackenzie, you love your children, whom you know so well, with a wonderful and real love."

10. Reflect on your experience of knowing and being known.

"WELL, THANKS, BUT I'm not that way with very many other people. My love tends to be pretty conditional most of the time."

11. What have your experiences of giving and receiving conditional and unconditional love been like?

"BUT IT'S A start, isn't it, Mackenzie? And you didn't move beyond your father's inability on your own—it was God and you together who changed you to love this way. And now you love your children much the way Father loves his."

Mack could feel his jaw involuntarily clench as he listened, and he felt the anger once more begin to rise. What should have been a reassuring commendation seemed more like a bitter pill that he now refused to swallow....

"Mackenzie," she encouraged, "is there something you would like to say?"

The silence left by her question now hung in the air. Mack struggled to retain his composure. He could hear his mother's advice ringing in his ears: "If you don't have anything nice to say, better to not speak at all."

"Uh...well, no! Not really."

"Mackenzie," she prompted, "this is not a time for your mother's common sense. This is a time for honesty, for truth. You don't believe that

Father loves his children very well, do you? You don't truly believe that God is good, do you?"

12. What is Mack experiencing and why?

13. Is it hard for you to be totally honest with God about certain things, especially anger at Him? Why?

"**Is Missy his** child?" Mack snapped.

"Of course!" she answered.

"Then no!" he blurted, rising to his feet. "I don't believe that God loves all of his children very well!"

He had said it, and now his accusation echoed off whatever walls surrounded the chamber. While Mack stood there, angry and ready to explode, the woman remained calm and unchanging in her demeanor. Slowly she rose from her high-backed chair, moving silently behind it and motioning him toward it. "Why don't you sit here?"

"Is that what honesty gets you, the hot seat?" he muttered, but he didn't move, he simply stared back at her.

"Mackenzie." She remained standing behind her chair. "Earlier I began to tell you why you are here today. Not only are you here because of your children, but you are here for judgment."

As the word echoed in the chamber, panic rose inside Mack like a swelling tide and slowly he sank into his chair. Instantly he felt guilty as memories spilled through his mind like rats fleeing the rising flood. He gripped the arms of his chair, trying to find some balance in the onslaught of images

and emotions. His failures as a human being suddenly loomed large, and
in the back of his mind he could almost hear a voice intoning his catalog
of sins, his dread deepening as the list grew longer and longer. He had no
defense. He was lost and he knew it.

14. What is Mack going through?

15. When do you feel the most shame or guilt? The most judged by God? Why?

"JUDGMENT? AND I'M not even dead?" A third time he stopped her, processing what he'd heard, anger replacing his panic. "This hardly seems fair!"
He knew his emotions were not helping. "Does this happen to other people—getting judged, I mean, before they're even dead? What if I change?
What if I do better the rest of my life? What if I repent? What then?"

"Is there something you wish to repent of, Mackenzie?" she asked,
unfazed by his outburst.

Mack slowly sat back down. He looked at the smooth surface of the
floor and then shook his head before answering. "I wouldn't know where to
begin," he mumbled. "I'm quite a mess, aren't I?"

"Yes, you are." Mack looked up and she smiled back. "You are a glorious,
destructive mess, Mackenzie, but you are not here to repent, at least not in
the way you understand. Mackenzie, you are not here to be judged."

"But," he said, "I thought you said that I was..."

"Here for judgment?" She remained cool and placid as a summer breeze
as she finished his question. "I did. But *you* are not on trial here."

Mack took a deep breath, relieved at her words.

"You will be the judge!"

16. Would you have the same misunderstanding as Mack? Why?

"WHAT? ME? I'D rather not." He paused. "I don't have any ability to judge."

"Oh, that is not true," returned the quick reply, tinged now with a hint of sarcasm. "You have already proven yourself very capable, even in our short time together. And besides, you have judged many throughout your life. You have judged the actions and even the motivations of others, as if you somehow knew what those were in truth. You have judged the color of skin and body language and body odor. You have judged history and relationships. You have even judged the value of a person's life by the quality of your concept of beauty. By all accounts, you are quite well practiced in the activity."

Mack felt shame reddening his face. He had to admit he had done an awful lot of judging in his time. But he was no different from anyone else, was he? Who doesn't jump to conclusions about others from the way they impact us. There it was again—his self-centered view of the world around him. He looked up and saw her peering intently at him and quickly looked down again.

"Tell me," she inquired, "if I may ask, on what criteria do you base your judgments?"

17. On what do you base your judgments?

"GOD"—SHE PAUSED—"AND THE human race." She said it as if it was of no particular consequence. It simply rolled off her tongue, as if this were a daily occurrence.

Mack was dumbfounded. "You have got to be kidding!" he exclaimed.

"Why not? Surely there are many people in your world you think deserve judgment. There must be at least a few who are to blame for so much of the pain and suffering. What about the greedy who feed off the poor of the world? What about the ones who sacrifice their young children to war? What about the men who beat their wives, Mackenzie? What about the fathers who beat their sons for no reason but to assuage their own suffering? Don't they deserve judgment, Mackenzie?"

Mack could sense the depths of his unresolved anger rising like a flood of fury. He sank back into the chair trying to maintain his balance against an onslaught of images, but he could feel his control ebbing away. His stomach knotted as he clenched his fists, his breathing coming short and quick.

"And what about the man who preys on innocent little girls? What about him, Mackenzie? Is that man guilty? Should he be judged?"

"Yes!" screamed Mack. "Damn him to hell!"

"Is he to blame for your loss?"

"Yes!"

"What about his father, the man who twisted his son into a terror, what about him?"

"Yes, him too!"

"How far do we go back, Mackenzie? This legacy of brokenness goes all the way back to Adam—what about him? But why stop there? What about God? God started this whole thing. Is God to blame?"

Mack was reeling. He didn't feel like a judge at all, but rather the one on trial.

The woman was unrelenting. "Isn't this where you are stuck, Mackenzie? Isn't this what fuels *The Great Sadness*? That God cannot be trusted? Surely, a father like you can judge *the* Father!"

Again his anger rose like a towering flame. He wanted to lash out, but she was right and there was no point in denying it.

She continued, "Isn't that your just complaint, Mackenzie? That God has failed you, that he failed Missy? That before the creation, God knew that one day your Missy would be brutalized, and still he created? And then he *allowed* that twisted soul to snatch her from your loving arms when he had the power to stop him. Isn't God to blame, Mackenzie?"

Mack was looking at the floor, a flurry of images pulling his emotions in every direction. Finally he said it, louder than he intended, and pointed his finger right at her. "Yes! God is to blame!" The accusation hung in the room as the gavel fell in his heart.

18. **Reflect on the emotion and intensity of this passage. Allow Wisdom to help you search your own thoughts and feelings of anger, resentment, and judgment.**

19. What is your "just complaint"?

"THEN," SHE SAID with finality, "if you are able to judge God so easily, you certainly can judge the world." Again she spoke without emotion. "You must choose two of your children to spend eternity in God's new heavens and new earth, but only two."

"What?" he erupted, turning to her in disbelief.

"And you must choose three of your children to spend eternity in hell."

Mack couldn't believe what he was hearing and started to panic.

"Mackenzie." Her voice now came as calm and wonderful as he had first heard it. "I am only asking you to do something that you believe God does. He knows every person ever conceived, and he knows them so much more deeper and clearer than you will ever know your own children. He loves each one according to his knowledge of the being of that son or daughter. You believe he will condemn most to an eternity of torment, away from his presence and apart from his love. Is that not true?"

20. What do you believe about God the judge?

"I CAN'T. I can't. I won't!" he screamed, and now the words and emotions came tumbling out. The woman just stood watching and waiting. Finally he looked at her, pleading with his eyes. "Could I go instead? If you need someone to torture for eternity, I'll go in their place. Would that work? Could I do that?" He fell at her feet, crying and begging now. "Please let me go for my children. Please, I would be happy to...Please, I am begging you. Please...Please..."

"Mackenzie, Mackenzie," she whispered, and her words came like a splash of cool water on a brutally hot day. Her hands gently touched his cheeks as she lifted him to his feet. Looking at her through blurring tears, he could see that her smile was radiant. "Now you sound like Jesus. You have judged well, Mackenzie. I am so proud of you!"

"But I haven't judged anything," Mack offered in confusion.

"Oh, but you have. You have judged them worthy of love, even if it costs you everything."

21. **Reflect on how you would respond in this situation. What insight does that give you about the Father, Son, and Holy Spirit?**

"I UNDERSTAND JESUS' love, but God is another story. I don't find them to be alike at all."

22. **How do you see God and Jesus differently?**

"No, SHE DIDN'T. She doesn't stop a lot of things that cause her pain. Your world is severely broken. You demanded your independence, and now you are angry with the One who loved you enough to give it to you. Nothing is as it should be, as Papa desires it to be, and as it will be one day. Right now your world is lost in darkness and chaos, and horrible things happen to those she is especially fond of."

23. **Reflect on the darkness and chaos of this fallen world.**

"FOR LOVE. SHE chose the way of the cross, where mercy triumphs over justice because of love. Would you instead prefer she'd chosen justice for everyone? Do you want justice, 'Dear Judge'?" And she smiled as she said it.

"No, I don't," he said as he lowered his head. "Not for me, and not for my children."

24. Reflect on mercy and justice.

"BUT I STILL don't understand why Missy had to die."

"She didn't have to, Mackenzie. This was no plan of Papa's. Papa has never needed evil to accomplish her good purposes."

25. Reflect on how evil fits into God's plan.

"BUT IT HURTS so much. There must be a better way."

"There is. You just can't see it now. Return from your independence, Mackenzie. Give up being her judge and know Papa for who she is. Then you will be able to embrace her love in the midst of your pain, instead of pushing her away with your self-centered perception of how you think the universe should be. Papa has crawled inside of your world to be with you, to be with Missy."

Mack stood up from the chair. "I don't want to be a judge anymore. I really do want to trust Papa." Unnoticed by Mack, the room lightened yet again as he moved around the table toward the simple chair where it all began. "But I'll need help."

She reached out and hugged Mack. "Now that sounds like the start of the trip home, Mackenzie. It certainly does."

26. Reflect on your independence—that part of you that struggles against God and wants the universe on your terms.

"**SHE KNOWS THAT** you are here, but she cannot see you. From her side, she is looking at the beautiful waterfall and nothing more. But she knows you are behind it."

"Waterfalls!" Mack exclaimed, laughing to himself. "She just can't get enough of waterfalls!" Now Mack focused on her, trying to memorize again every detail of her expression and hair and hands. As he did so, Missy's face erupted in a huge smile, dimples standing out. In slow motion, with great exaggeration, he could see her mouth the words, "It's okay, I"—and now she signed the words—"love you."

Mack watched every move his precious Missy was making. "Has she forgiven me?" he asked.

"Forgiven you for what?"

"I failed her," he whispered…. "I didn't stop him from taking her. He took her while I wasn't paying attention…" His voice trailed off.

"If you remember, you were saving your son. Only you, in the entire universe, believe that somehow you are to blame. Missy doesn't believe that, neither does Nan or Papa. Perhaps it's time to let that go—that lie. And Mackenzie, even if you had been to blame, her love is much stronger than your fault could ever be."

27. Reflections.

"**IS IT OVER?**" he asked.

"For now," she replied tenderly. "Mackenzie, judgment is not about destruction, but about setting things right."

28. Reflect again on judgment.

In the Belly of the Beasts

Identity, Reality, Presence,
and Learning to Live Loved

For the past years it had defined for him what was normal, but now unexpectedly it had vanished. *Normal is a myth,* he thought to himself.

The Great Sadness would not be part of his identity any longer.

1. **What has become a part of your identity that God may be inviting you to let go of?**

"**Hey, I think** my best was thirteen skips," he said as he laughed and walked to meet Mack. "But Tyler beat me by three and Josh threw one that skipped so fast we all lost count." As they hugged, Jesus added, "You have special kids, Mack. You and Nan have loved them very well. Kate is struggling, as you know, but we're not done there."

The very ease and intimacy with which Jesus talked about his children touched him deeply.

2. **Reflect on Jesus' ability to love well those you care about. You are not alone in your love and concern for them.**

"**BUT AS FOR** 'Is any of this real?' Far more real than you can imagine." Jesus paused for a moment to get Mack's full attention. "A better question might be, 'What is real?'"

"I'm beginning to think that I have no idea," Mack offered.

"Would all this be any less 'real' if it were inside a dream?"

"I think I'd be disappointed."

"Why? Mack, there is far more going on here than you have the ability to perceive. Let me assure you, all of this is very much real, far more real than life as you've known it."

3. **Reflect on Mack's struggle and your own struggle with what is real and what is "more real than life as you've known it."**

JESUS REACHED OVER and put his hand on Mack's shoulder and squeezed. Gently he spoke, "Mack, she was never alone. I never left her; we never left her, not for one instant. I could no more abandon her, or you, than I could abandon myself."

4. **Reflect on pain, suffering, and trauma. Where was God, and how did God respond during times such as this in your life? Consider for a moment that this intimate God of love (versus other images, core beliefs, or gods) is with you through all the ups and downs, even trauma and death.**

"**SHE MAY HAVE** been only six years old, but Missy and I are friends. We talk. She had no idea what was going to happen. She was actually more worried about you and the other kids, knowing you couldn't find her. She prayed for you, for your peace."

Mack wept, fresh tears rolling down his cheeks. This time, he didn't mind. Jesus gently pulled him into his arms and held him.... The tears flowed freely now, but even Mack noticed this time it was different. He was no longer alone. Without embarrassment he wept onto the shoulder of this man he had grown to love. With each sob he felt the tension drain away, replaced by a deep sense of relief. Finally, he took a deep breath and blew it out as he lifted his head.

5. Compare Mack's *Great Sadness* to what is happening in this scene.

6. Have you ever experienced this kind of sacred moment with a loving and present God? Take some time to reflect on that experience and to share your current hurts, pain, anger, and/or joy with God.

THEN, WITHOUT ANOTHER word, he stood up, slung his shoes over one shoulder, and simply walked into the water. Although he was a little surprised when his first step found the lake bottom up to his ankles, he didn't care....

"This always works better when we do it together, don't you think?" Jesus asked, smiling....

What mattered was that Jesus was with him. Perhaps he was beginning to trust him after all, even if it were only in baby steps.

7. Reflections.

"THE DARKNESS HIDES the true size of fears and lies and regrets," Jesus explained. "The truth is they are more shadow than reality, so they seem bigger in the dark. When the light shines into the places where they live inside you, you start to see them for what they are."

"But why do we keep all that crap inside?" Mack asked.

"Because we believe it's safer there. And, sometimes, when you're a kid trying to survive, it really is safer there. Then you grow up on the outside, but on the inside you're still that kid in the dark cave surrounded by monsters, and out of habit you keep adding to your collection. We all collect things we value, you know?"

8. Reflect on this passage and the things you have hidden in your heart.

"So, HOW DOES that change, you know, for somebody who's lost in the dark like me?"

"Most often, pretty slowly," Jesus answered. "Remember, you can't do it alone. Some folks try with all kinds of coping mechanisms and mental games. But the monsters are still there, just waiting for the chance to come out."

"So what do I do now?"

"What you're already doing, Mack—learning to live loved. It's not an easy concept for humans. You have a hard time sharing anything." He chuckled and continued, "So, yes, what we desire is for you to 're-turn' to us, and then we come and make our home inside you, and then we share. The friendship is real, not merely imagined. We're meant to experience this life, your life, together, in a dialogue, sharing the journey."

9. Reflect on being lost in the dark, mental games, monsters, and learning to live loved.

"CAN I ASK, why didn't you tell me about Missy earlier, like last night, or a year ago, or...?"

"Don't think we didn't try. Have you noticed that in your pain you assume the worst of me? I've been talking to you for a long time, but today was the first time you could hear it, and all those other times weren't a waste either. Like little cracks in the wall, one at a time but woven together they prepared you for today. You have to take the time to prepare the soil if you want it to embrace the seed."

10. Reflect on this in your life in the light of identity, reality, the presence of God, and learning to live loved.

"IT'S ALL PART of the timing of grace, Mack," Jesus continued. "If the universe contained only one human being, timing would be rather simple. But add just one more, and, well, you know the story. Each choice ripples out through time and relationships, bouncing off other choices. And out of what seems to be a huge mess, Papa weaves a magnificent tapestry. Only Papa can work all this out, and she does it with grace."

"So I guess all I can do is follow her," Mack concluded.

"Yup, that's the point. Now you're beginning to understand what it means to be truly human."

11. Reflect on who God is and what it means to be truly human.

"WAS I SEEING heaven when I was seeing Missy? It looked a lot like here."

"Well, Mack, our final destiny is not the picture of heaven that you have stuck in your head—you know, the image of pearly gates and streets of gold. Instead, it's a new cleansing of this universe, so it will indeed look a lot like here."

12. Read and reflect on some of the passages in the Bible about the reality of heaven.

"THEN WHAT'S WITH the pearly-gates-and-gold stuff?"

"That stuff, my brother," Jesus began, lying back on the dock and closing his eyes against the warmth and brightness of the day, "is a picture of me and the woman I'm in love with…. It is a picture of my bride, the church: individuals who together form a spiritual city with a living river flowing through the middle, and on both shores trees growing with fruit that will heal the hurt and sorrows of the nations. And this city is always open, and each gate into it is made of a single pearl…" He opened one eye and looked at Mack. "That would be me!" He saw Mack's question and explained, "Pearls, Mack. The only precious stone made by pain, suffering, and—finally—death."

"You're talking about the church as this woman you're in love with; I'm pretty sure I haven't met her." He turned away slightly. "She's not the place I go on Sundays," Mack said, more to himself, unsure if that was safe to say out loud.

"Mack, that's because you're seeing only the institution, a man-made system. That's not what I came to build. What I see are people and their lives, a living, breathing community of all those who love me, not buildings and programs."

13. Reflect on the bride of Christ versus the institution of the church.

"IT'S SIMPLE, MACK. It's all about relationships and simply sharing life. What we are doing right now—just doing this—and being open and available to others around us. My church is all about people, and life is all about relationships. *You* can't build it. It's my job, and I'm actually pretty good at it," Jesus said with a chuckle.

For Mack these words were like a breath of fresh air! Simple. Not a bunch of exhausting work and a long list of demands, and not sitting in endless meetings staring at the backs of people's heads, people he really didn't even know. Just sharing life.

14. Where is your church not the institution, but the place where you are open and available to others and simply share life together?

"I REALLY DO want to understand. I mean, I find you so different from all the well-intentioned religious stuff I'm familiar with."

"As well-intentioned as it might be, you know that religious machinery can chew up people!" Jesus said with a bite of his own. "An awful lot of what is done in my name has nothing to do with me and is often, even if unintentional, very contrary to my purposes."

15. Reflect on "well-intentioned religious stuff" and what upsets Jesus.

"YOU'RE NOT TOO fond of religion and institutions?" Mack said, not sure if he was asking a question or making an observation.

"I don't create institutions—never have, never will."

"What about the institution of marriage?"

"Marriage is not an institution. It's a relationship." Jesus paused, his voice steady and patient. "Like I said, I don't create institutions; that's an occupation for those who want to play God."

16. Do you agree or disagree with the idea that God does not create institutions? Why?

17. What happens to relationships in institutions or large systems?

NOTICING THAT MACK'S eyes were glazing over, Jesus downshifted. "Put simply, these terrors are tools that many use to prop up their illusions of security and control. People are afraid of uncertainty, afraid of the future. These institutions, these structures and ideologies, are all a vain effort to create some sense of certainty and security where there isn't any. It's all false! Systems cannot provide you security, only I can."

18. Reflect on your own need for security and how you try to achieve it.

"I DON'T HAVE an agenda here, Mack. Just the opposite," Jesus said. "I came to give you life to the fullest. My life." Mack was still straining to understand. "The simplicity and purity of enjoying a growing friendship?"

"Uh, got it!"

"If you try to live this without me, without the ongoing dialogue of us sharing this journey together, it will be like trying to walk on the water by yourself. You can't! And when you try, however well intentioned, you're going to sink."

19. Reflect on your own growing friendships with others and with Christ as you learn to live loved.

"THAT'S ALL I ask of you. When you start to sink, let me rescue you."

It seemed like a simple request, but Mack was used to being the life-guard, not the one drowning. "Jesus, I'm not sure I know how to—"

"Let me show you. Just keep giving me the little bit you have, and together we'll watch it grow."

20. What makes this hard for you to do?

"I HAVE BEEN told so many lies," he admitted.

Jesus looked at him and then with one arm pulled Mack in and hugged him. "I know, Mack, so have I. I just didn't believe them."

21. What are the lies you have believed about yourself and about God?

"MACK, THE WORLD system is what it is. Institutions, systems, ideologies, and all the vain, futile efforts of humanity that go with them are everywhere, and interaction with all of it is unavoidable. But I can give you freedom to overcome any system of power in which you find yourself, be it religious, economic, social, or political. You will grow in the freedom to be inside or outside all kinds of systems and to move freely between and among them. Together, you and I can be in it and not of it."

22. Reflect on growing in this kind of freedom in your own life.

"MACK, I LOVE them. And you wrongly judge many of them. For those who are both in it and of it, we must find ways to love and serve them, don't you think?" asked Jesus. "Remember, the people who know me are the ones who are free to live and love without any agenda."

23. Reflect on judging versus loving with no agenda.

"**THOSE WHO LOVE** me have come from every system that exists. They were Buddhists or Mormons, Baptists or Muslims; some are Democrats, some Republicans, and many don't vote or are not part of any Sunday morning or religious institutions. I have followers who were murderers and many who were self-righteous. Some are bankers and bookies, Americans and Iraqis, Jews and Palestinians. I have no desire to make them Christian, but I do want to join them in their transformation into sons and daughters of my Papa, into my brothers and sisters, into my Beloved."

24. **This statement may be very hard for some. Take time to prayerfully reflect on what it means to be a "Christian" versus being in a beloved relationship with the Triune God.**

"**DOES THAT MEAN,**" said Mack, "that all roads will lead to you?"

"Not at all." Jesus smiled as he reached for the door handle to the shop. "Most roads don't lead anywhere. What it does mean is that I will travel any road to find you."

25. **Reflections.**

A MEETING OF HEARTS

Suffering, Lies, Evil, and the Scared Space of Independence

AS MACK ATE another scone he groped for the courage to speak his heart. "Papa?" he asked, and for the first time calling God "Papa" did not seem awkward to him.

"Yes, Mack?" she answered as her eyes opened and she smiled with delight.

"I've been pretty hard on you."

"Hmmmm, Sophia must've gotten to you."

"Did she ever! I had no idea I had presumed to be your judge. It sounds so horribly arrogant."

"That's because it was," Papa responded with a smile.

"I am so sorry. I really had no idea..." Mack shook his head sadly.

"But that is in the past now, where it belongs. I don't even want your sorrow for it, Mack. I just want us to grow on together without it."

"I want that too," Mack said.

1. **Reflect on connecting or reconnecting with God in this richly personal way. Focus specifically on the statement, "But that is in the past now, where it belongs. I don't even want your sorrow for it, Mack. I just want us to grow on together without it."**

"IS THAT WHAT this is about? Did she have to die so you could change me?"

"Whoa there, Mack." Papa leaned forward. "That's not how I do things."

"But she loved that story so much."

"Of course she did. That's how she came to appreciate what Jesus did for her and the whole human race. Stories about a person willing to exchange his or her life for another's are a golden thread in your world, revealing both your need and my heart."

"But if she hadn't died, I wouldn't be here now..."

"Mack, just because I work incredible good out of unspeakable tragedies doesn't mean I orchestrate the tragedies. Don't ever assume that my using something means I caused it or that I needed it to accomplish my purposes. That will only lead you to false notions about me. Grace doesn't depend on suffering to exist, but where there is suffering you will find grace in many facets and colors."

2. Reflect on the way God works in and through grace and suffering.

"BUT I ALWAYS liked Jesus better than you. He seemed so gracious and you seemed so..."

"Mean? Sad, isn't it? He came to show people who I am and most folks believe the qualities he portrayed were unique to him. They still play us off like good cop/bad cop most of the time, especially the religious folk. When they want people to do what they think is right, they need a stern God. When they need forgiveness, they run to Jesus."

3. Reflections.

"BECAUSE THAT IS what love does," answered Papa. "Remember, Mackenzie, I don't wonder what you will do or what choices you will make. I already know. Let's say, for example, I am trying to teach you how not to hide inside lies—hypothetically, of course," she said with a wink. "And let's say that I know it will take you forty-seven situations and events before you will actually hear me—that is, before you will hear clearly enough to agree with me and change. So when you don't hear me the first time, I'm not frustrated or disappointed, I'm thrilled. Only forty-six more times to go! And that first time will be a building block to construct a bridge of healing that one day—that today—you will walk across."

4. How does this match or differ from your concept of how God works?

"OKAY, NOW I'M feeling guilty," he admitted.

"Let me know how that works for you." Papa chuckled. "Seriously, Mackenzie, it's not about feeling guilty. Guilt'll never help you find freedom in me. The best it can do is make you try harder to conform to some ethic on the outside. I'm about the inside."

5. What has been your experience with guilt? How does it work in your life? How does God use or deal with guilt?

"BUT, WHAT YOU said, I mean, about hiding inside lies. I guess I've done that one way or another most of my life."

"Honey, you're a survivor. No shame in that. Your daddy hurt you something fierce. Life hurt you. Lies are one of the easiest places for survivors to run. They give you a sense of safety, a place where you only have to depend on yourself. But it's a dark place, isn't it?"

"So dark," Mack muttered with a shake of his head.

"But are you willing to give up the power and safety it promises you? That's the question."

"What do you mean?" asked Mack, looking up at her.

"Lies are a little fortress; inside them you can feel safe and powerful. Through your little fortress of lies you try to run your life and manipulate others. But the fortress needs walls, so you build some. These are the justifications for your lies. You know, like you are doing this to protect someone you love, to keep them from feeling pain. Whatever works, just so you feel okay about the lies."

6. **What are the walls you protect yourself with and sometimes hide behind?**

"SEE? THERE YOU go, Mackenzie, justifying yourself. What you just said is a bold-faced lie, but you can't see it." She leaned forward. "Do you want me to tell you what the truth is?"

7. **Do you want to hear the truth from God? Reflect on your self-justification and the truth God is trying to speak into your life.**

"THE REAL REASON was that you were afraid of having to deal with the emotions you might have encountered, both from her and in yourself. Emotions scare you, Mack. You lied to protect yourself, not her!"

He sat back. Papa was absolutely right.

"And furthermore," she continued, "such a lie is unloving. In the name of caring about her, your lie became an inhibitor in your relationship with her, and in her relationship with me. If you had told her, maybe she would be here with us now."

8. **What are some of the things you do to protect yourself or others? How might those things actually be inhibiting your relationship with them and with God?**

"YOU TELL HER, Mackenzie. You face the fear of coming out of the dark and tell her, and you ask for her forgiveness and let her forgiveness heal you. Ask her to pray for you, Mack. Take the risks of honesty. When you mess up again, ask for forgiveness again. It's a process, honey, and life is real enough without having to be obscured by lies. And remember, I am bigger than your lies. I can work beyond them. But that doesn't make them right or stop the damage they do or the hurt they cause others."

9. **Who do you need to be more honest and open with? Reflect on the risk of honesty and the healing of forgiveness in the relationships of your life.**

"WHAT IF SHE doesn't forgive me?" Mack knew that this was indeed a very deep fear that he lived with. It felt safer to continue to throw new lies on the growing pile of old ones.

"Ah, that is the risk of faith, Mack. Faith does not grow in the house of certainty. I am not here to tell you that Nan will forgive you. Perhaps she won't or can't, but my life inside you will appropriate risk and uncertainty to transform you by your own choices into a truth teller, and that will be a miracle greater than raising the dead."

10. **Can you identify with Mack's fear of not being forgiven by someone? Reflect on "the risk of faith" and being a "truth teller."**

"BUT I'VE TRIED pretty hard to lock you out of my life."

"People are tenacious when it comes to the treasure of their imaginary independence. They hoard and hold their sickness with a firm grip. They find their identity and worth in their brokenness and guard it with every ounce of strength they have. No wonder grace has such little attraction. In that sense you have tried to lock the door of your heart from the inside."

11. **Reflect on your "imaginary independence" and identity. What areas of your heart are you trying to lock God out of? Why?**

"**BUT IF** I understand what you're saying, the consequences of our selfishness are part of the process that brings us to the end of our delusions and helps us find you. Is that why you don't stop every evil? Is that why you didn't warn me that Missy was in danger or help us find her?" The accusing tone was no longer in Mack's voice.

"If only it were that simple, Mackenzie. Nobody knows what horrors I have saved the world from 'cause people can't see what never happened. All evil flows from independence, and independence is your choice. If I were to simply revoke all the choices of independence, the world as you know it would cease to exist and love would have no meaning. This world is not a playground where I keep all my children free from evil. Evil is the chaos of this age that you brought to me, but it will not have the final say. Now it touches everyone I love, those who follow me and those who don't. If I take away the consequences of people's choices, I destroy the possibility of love. Love that is forced is no love at all."

12. Reflect on why there is evil. Do you agree with the statement "Love that is forced is no love at all"?

"**HONEY, LET ME** tell you one of the reasons that it makes no sense to you. It's because you have such a small view of what it means to be human. You and this creation are incredible, whether you understand that or not. You are wonderful beyond imagination. Just because you make horrendous and destructive choices does not mean you deserve less respect for what you inherently are—the pinnacle of my creation and the center of my affection."

13. What do you believe regarding what it means to be human? Let yourself take in and reflect on the reality that you, not just humanity in general, but you are the pinnacle of God's creation and the center of God's affection.

"ALSO," SHE INTERRUPTED, "don't forget that in the midst of all your pain and heartache, you are surrounded by beauty, the wonder of creation, art, your music and culture, the sounds of laughter and love, of whispered hopes and celebrations, of new life and transformation, of reconciliation and forgiveness. These also are the results of your choices, and every choice matters, even the hidden ones. So whose choices should we countermand, Mackenzie?"

14. Reflections.

"YOU DEMAND YOUR independence, but then complain that I actually love you enough to give it to you."

15. In what areas of your life have you demanded your independence and then complained when God actually gave it to you?

"MACKENZIE, MY PURPOSES are not for my comfort, or yours. My purposes are always and only an expression of love. I purpose to work life out of death, to bring freedom out of brokenness and turn darkness into light. What you see as chaos, I see as a fractal. All things must unfold, even though it puts all those I love in the midst of a world of horrible tragedies—even the one closest to me."

16. Reflect on three things: 1) God's true purpose. 2) The purpose you fear God has. 3) The purpose you want God to have. What motivates each of those thoughts? Do you at your core, not just intellectually, believe that God's purposes are always and only an expression of love?

"**YUP, I LOVE** that boy." Papa looked away and shook her head. "Everything's about him, you know. One day you folk will understand what he gave up. There are just no words."

Mack could feel his own emotions welling up. Something touched him deeply as he watched Papa talk about her Son.

17. Reflections.

"**LIKE I SAID,** everything is about him. Creation and history are all about Jesus. He is the very center of our purpose, and in him we are now fully human, so our purpose and your destiny are forever linked. You might say that we have put all our eggs in the one human basket. There is no plan B."

"Seems pretty risky," Mack surmised.

"Maybe for you, but not for me. There has never been a question that what I wanted from the beginning, I will get." Papa sat forward and crossed her arms on the table. "Honey, you asked me what Jesus accomplished on the cross, so now listen to me carefully: through his death and resurrection, I am now fully reconciled to the world."

"The whole world? You mean those who believe in you, right?"

"The whole world, Mack. All I am telling you is that reconciliation is a two-way street, and I have done my part, totally, completely, finally. It is not the nature of love to force a relationship, but it is the nature of love to open the way."

18. Reflect on your relationship with God, reconciliation, and what Christ did to open the way.

VERBS AND OTHER FREEDOM

The Sacred Space of the Presence of God

...**HE DISCOVERED A** perfect spot to drift and watch the waterfall. Alpine flowers blossomed everywhere, adding splashes of color to the landscape. This was the most calm and consistent sense of peace that Mack had felt in ages—if ever.

1. **Why was Mack so calm and at peace? Have you experienced similar peace?**

HE SHOOK HIS head as he thought about his daughter, so tough but so fragile; he wondered how he might find a way to reach her heart. He was no longer surprised how easily tears could come to his eyes.

2. **Reflect on reaching someone's heart.**

"FOR YOU TO know or not," she explained, "has nothing at all to do with whether I am actually here or not. I am always with you; sometimes I want you to be aware in a special way—more intentional."

3. Reflect on this statement and your awareness of the Holy Spirit.

SARAYU SMILED. "MACKENZIE, you can always talk to me and I will always be with you, whether you sense my presence or not."

"I know that now, but how will I hear you?"

"You will learn to hear my thoughts in yours, Mackenzie," she reassured him.

"Will it be clear? What if I confuse you with another voice? What if I make mistakes?"

Sarayu laughed, the sound like tumbling water, only set to music. "Of course you will make mistakes; everybody makes mistakes, but you will begin to better recognize my voice as we continue to grow our relationship."

"I don't want to make mistakes," Mack grunted.

"Oh, Mackenzie," responded Sarayu, "mistakes are a part of life, and Papa works her purpose in them too."

4. Reflect on hearing and responding to the Holy Spirit, and reflect on making mistakes.

"SOMEHOW IT SEEMED easier to live with God when I thought of him as the demanding taskmaster, or even to cope with the loneliness of *The Great Sadness*."

"You think so?" she asked. "Really?"

"At least then I seemed to have things under control."

5. **Reflect. Why do we in general, and you specifically, want to "have things under control"?**

"I AM AFRAID of emotions," Mack admitted, a bit perturbed that she seemed to make light of it. "I don't like how they feel. I've hurt others with them and I can't trust them at all. Did you create all of them or only the good ones?"

6. **Reflect on your emotions. How would you answer Mack's question?**

"EMOTIONS ARE THE colors of the soul—they are spectacular and incredible. When you don't feel, the world becomes dull and colorless. Just think how *The Great Sadness* reduced the range of color in your life down to monotones and flat grays and blacks."

"So help me understand them," pleaded Mack.

"Not much to understand, actually. They just are. They are neither bad nor good; they just exist. Here is something that will help you sort this out in your mind, Mackenzie. *Paradigms power perception and perceptions power emotions.* Most emotions are responses to perception—what you think is true about a given situation. If your perception is false, then your emotional response to it will be false too. So check your perceptions, and beyond that check the truthfulness of your paradigms—what you believe. Just because you believe something firmly doesn't make it true. Be willing to reexamine what you believe. The more you live in the truth, the more your emotions will help you see clearly. But even then, you don't want to trust them more than me."

7. **Think about a situation in your life that triggered strong emotion. (Maybe even take some time to journal about it.) Reflect first on the emotion. Now explore your perceptions of the situation at the time and how they powered the emotion. What are your underlying beliefs (paradigms) that fuel those perceptions? To see our paradigms, like foundation stones in a house, is not always easy. Ask the Holy Spirit to help you see them clearly. When you begin uncovering and inspecting foundation stones, it can make the whole house feel unsteady. Trust the Holy Spirit to help you set things right.**

"It feels like living out of relationship—you know, trusting and talking to you—is a bit more complicated than just following rules."

"What rules are those, Mackenzie?"

"You know, all the things the Scriptures tell us we should do."

"Okay..." she said with some hesitation. "And what might those be?"

"You know," he answered sarcastically. "About doing good things and avoiding evil, being kind to the poor, reading your Bible, praying, and going to church. Things like that."

"I see. And how is that working for you?"

8. **Rules or relationship. How is that working out for you?**

"**MACKENZIE!**" **SHE CHIDED,** her words flowing with affection. "The Bible doesn't teach you to follow rules. It is a picture of Jesus. While words may tell you what God is like and even what he may want from you, you cannot do any of it on your own. Life and living are *in him* and in no other. My goodness, you didn't think you could live the righteousness of God on your own, did you?"

"Well, I thought so, sorta..." he said sheepishly. "But you gotta admit, rules and principles are simpler than relationships."

"It is true that relationships are a whole lot messier than rules, but rules will never give you answers to the deep questions of the heart and they will never love you."

9. **Reflect on how you feel when you are trying to follow rules versus what you do when you feel the love of God. Which of those two situations results in more right living?**

"**MACKENZIE, RELIGION IS** about having the right answers, and some of its answers are right. But I am about the process that takes you to the *living answer* and once you get to him, he will change you from the inside. There are a lot of smart people who are able to say a lot of right things from their brains because they have been told what the right answers are, but they don't know me at all."

10. **Now reflect on not just rules versus relationship, but being right versus relationship.**

"**OF COURSE. YOU** might see me in a piece of art, or music, or silence, or through people, or in creation, or in your joy and sorrow. My ability to communicate is limitless, living and transforming, and it will always be tuned to Papa's goodness and love. And you will hear and see me in the Bible in fresh ways. Just don't look for rules and principles; look for relationship—a way of coming to be with us."

11. **How and where do you see God? What are you looking for, rules and principles or relationship?**

AS MACK ATE, he listened to the banter between the three. They talked and laughed like old friends who knew one another intimately. As he thought about it, that was assuredly more true for his hosts than anyone inside or outside creation. He was envious of the carefree but respectful conversation and wondered what it would take to share that with Nan and maybe even with some friends.

12. **Reflect on the intimacy, the oneness of the Trinity. What would it take to share that in your most intimate relationships? What gets in the way of this kind of intimacy?**

"**I GUESS WHAT** I want to ask is, why do you love me, when I have nothing to offer you?"

"If you think about it, Mack," Jesus answered, "it should be very freeing to know that you can offer us nothing, at least not anything that can add or take away from who we are…That should alleviate any pressure to perform."

"And do you love your own children more when they perform well?" added Papa.

"No, I see your point." Mack paused. "But I do feel more fulfilled because they are in my life—do you?"

"No," said Papa. "We are already fully fulfilled within ourselves. You are designed to be in community as well, made as you are in our very image. So for you to feel that way about your children, or anything that 'adds' to you, is perfectly natural and right."

13. Why are you loved by God? By others?

"**WHAT DO YOU** expect of me now?"

"Let me answer that by asking you a question. Why do you think we came up with the Ten Commandments?"

14. What does God expect of you, and why did God come up with the Ten Commandments?

"**IF THAT WERE** true, which it is not," Sarayu countered, "then how many do you think lived righteously enough to enter our good graces?"

"Not very many, if people are like me," Mack observed.

"Actually, only one succeeded—Jesus. He not only obeyed the letter of the Law but fulfilled the spirit of it completely. But understand this, Mackenzie—to do that he had to rest fully and dependently upon me."

"Then why did you give us those commandments?" asked Mack.

"Actually, we wanted you to give up trying to be righteous on your own. It was a mirror to reveal just how filthy your face gets when you live independently."

"But as I'm sure you know, there are many," responded Mack, "who think they are made righteous by following the rules."

"But can you clean your face with the same mirror that shows you how dirty you are? There is no mercy or grace in rules, not even for one mistake.

That's why Jesus fulfilled all of it for you—so that it no longer has juris-
diction over you. And the Law that once contained impossible demands—
'Thou shall not…'—actually becomes a promise we fulfill in you."

**15. Reflect on "the Law" as demands to live up to, a mirror to see the filth
we are covered in, and a promise Christ has fulfilled in us.**

"**ARE YOU SAYING** I don't have to follow the rules?" Mack had now completely stopped eating and was concentrating on the conversation.

"Yes. In Jesus you are not under any law. All things are lawful."

"You can't be serious! You're messing with me again," moaned Mack.

"Child," said Papa, "you ain't heard nuthin' yet."

"Mackenzie," Sarayu continued, "those who are afraid of freedom are
those who cannot trust us to live in them. Trying to keep the Law is actually
a declaration of independence, a way of keeping control."

**16. Reflect on fear of freedom and trusting God to live in you versus try-
ing to keep the rules as a way to maintain a sense of control. How do
you declare your freedom from God rather than finding your freedom in relationship with God?**

"**IS THAT WHY** we like the law so much—to give us some control?" asked
Mack.

"It is much worse than that," resumed Sarayu. "It grants you the power
to judge others and feel superior to them. You believe you are living to a
higher standard than those you judge. Enforcing rules, especially in more
subtle expressions like responsibility and expectation, is a vain attempt to
create certainty out of uncertainty. And contrary to what you might think,

I have a great fondness for uncertainty. Rules cannot bring freedom; they have only the power to accuse."

"Whoa!" Mack suddenly realized what Sarayu had said. "Are you telling me that responsibility and expectation are just another form of rules we are no longer under? Did I hear you right?"

17. **Reflect on responsibility and expectation in your life. Do they ever become unwritten rules? How do those unwritten rules impact your freedom and your relationships?**

"**THEN LET'S USE** your two words: *responsibility* and *expectation*. Before your words became nouns, they were first my words, nouns with movement and experience buried inside them: the ability to respond and expectancy. My words are alive and dynamic—full of life and possibility; yours are dead, full of law and fear and judgment. That is why you won't find the word *responsibility* in the Scriptures.... Religion must use law to empower itself and control the people needed in order to survive. I give you an ability to respond and your response is to be free to love and serve in every situation, and therefore each moment is different and unique and wonderful. Because I am your ability to respond, I have to be present in you. If I simply gave you a *responsibility*, I would not have to be with you at all. It would now be a task to perform, an obligation to be met, something to fail."

"Oh, boy, oh, boy," Mack said again, without much enthusiasm.

"Let's use the example of friendship and how removing the element of life from a noun can drastically alter a relationship. Mack, if you and I are friends, there is an expectancy that exists within our relationship. When we see each other or are apart, there is an expectancy of being together, of laughing and talking. That expectancy has no concrete definition; it is alive and dynamic and everything that emerges from our being together is a unique gift shared by no one else. But what happens if I change that expectancy to an *expectation*—spoken or unspoken? Suddenly, law has entered into our relationship. You are now expected to perform in a way that meets my expectations. Our living friendship rapidly deteriorates into a dead thing with rules and requirements. It is no longer about you and me, but about what friends are supposed to do, or the responsibilities of a good friend."

"Or," noted Mack, "the responsibilities of a husband, or a father, or employee, or whatever. I get the picture. I would much rather live in expectancy."

18. Reflect on the difference between responsiveness and responsibility, expectancy and expectations.

"BUT," ARGUED MACK, "if you didn't have expectations and responsibilities, wouldn't everything just fall apart?"

19. How would you answer Mack's question?

"ONLY IF YOU are of the world, apart from me, and under the law. Responsibilities and expectations are the basis of guilt and shame and judgment, and they provide the essential framework that promotes performance as the basis for identity and value."

20. Reflect on Sarayu's answer. How much is performance a basis for your sense of identity and value?

"**ARE YOU SAYING** you have no expectations of me?"

"...And beyond that, because I have no expectations, you never disappoint me."

"...Never!" Papa stated emphatically. "What I do have is a constant and living expectancy in our relationship, and I give you an ability to respond to any situation and circumstance in which you find yourself. To the degree that you resort to expectations and responsibilities, to that degree you neither know me nor trust me."

"And," added Jesus, "to that degree you will live in fear."

21. Talk with God about this in your life.

"**THE TROUBLE WITH** living by priorities," Sarayu said, "is that everything is seen as a hierarchy, a pyramid, and you and I have already had that discussion. If you put God at the top, what does that really mean, and how much is enough? How much time do you give me before you can go on about the rest of your day, the part that interests you so much more?"

Papa again interrupted. "You see, Mackenzie, I don't just want a piece of you and a piece of your life. Even if you were able, which you are not, to give me the biggest piece, that is not what I want. I want all of you and all of every part of you and your day."

Jesus now spoke again. "Mack, I don't want to be first among a list of values; I want to be at the center of everything. When I live in you, then together we can live through everything that happens to you. Rather than the top of a pyramid, I want to be the center of a mobile, where everything in your life—your friends, family, occupation, thoughts, activities—is connected to me but moves with the wind, in and out and back and forth, in an incredible dance of being."

"And I," concluded Sarayu, "I am the wind." She smiled and bowed.

22. Reflect on the "incredible dance of being" that God is inviting you to join.

"MACKENZIE, IF YOU would allow me, I would like to give you a gift for this evening. May I touch your eyes and heal them, just for tonight?"

Mack was surprised. "I see well enough, don't I?"

"Actually," Sarayu said apologetically, "you see very little, even though for a human you see fairly well. But just for tonight, I would love you to see a bit of what we see."

23. Reflect on and allow God to help you see what she sees in and around you.

A FESTIVAL OF FRIENDS

Holy and Majestic Sight, Seeing Face-to-Face

"IT IS ALL so incredibly beautiful," he whispered, surrounded as he was by such a holy and majestic sight.

1. Reflect on holy and majestic sights God has allowed you to see.

HE DREW IT back, startled, as he realized that he too was ablaze. He looked at his hands, wonderfully crafted and clearly visible inside the cascading colors of light that seemed to glove them. He examined the rest of his body to find that light and color robed him completely: a clothing of purity that allowed him both freedom and propriety.

Mack realized also that he felt no pain, not even in his usually aching joints. In fact, he had never felt this well, this whole.

2. Is this Mack seeing how he will be or who he truly is? Reflect on seeing yourself the way you truly are.

THEY BROKE INTO the meadow, an army of children. There were no candles—they themselves were lights. And within their own radiance, each was dressed in a distinctive garb that Mack imagined represented every tribe and tongue. He could identify only a few, but it didn't matter. These were the children of the earth, Papa's children. They entered with quiet dignity and grace, faces full of contentment and peace, young ones holding the hands of even younger ones.

3. Reflect on this and other passages in this chapter that depict the spiritual world. How would you describe the spiritual world around us? How would you describe heaven?

"HERE, WE ARE able to *see* one another truly, and part of *seeing* means that individual personality and emotion are visible in color and light."

> We don't yet see things clearly. We're squinting in a fog, peering through a mist. But it won't be long before the weather clears and the sun shines bright! We'll see it all then, see it all as clearly as God sees us, knowing him directly just as he knows us! But for right now, until that completeness, we have three things to do to lead us toward that consummation: Trust steadily in God, hope unswervingly, love extravagantly. And the best of the three is love.
>
> 1 CORINTHIANS 13:12–13 MSG

4. How does this impact your view of heaven, the spiritual world, yourself, and others? (For extra reading, consider C. S. Lewis's book *The Weight of Glory*.)

"**PERHAPS THE BEST** way you can understand is for me to give you a quick illustration. Suppose, Mack, that you are hanging out with a friend at your local coffee shop. You are focused on your companion and if you had eyes to see, the two of you would be enveloped in an array of colors and light, which mark not only your uniqueness as individuals but also the uniqueness of the relationship between you and the emotions you'd be experiencing in that moment."

"But—" Mack began to ask, only to be cut off.

"But suppose," Sarayu went on, "that another person you love enters the coffee shop, and although you are wrapped up in the conversation with your first friend, you notice this other's entry. Again, if you had eyes to see the greater reality, here is what you would witness: as you continued your current conversation, a unique combination of color and light would leave you and wrap itself around the one who had just entered, representing you in another form of loving and greeting that one. And one more thing, Mackenzie: it is not only visual but sensual as well. You can feel, smell, and even taste that uniqueness."

5. Reflections.

"**THE ONE HAVING** so much trouble containing himself—that one—is your father."

A wave of emotions, a mixture of anger and longings, washed over Mack, and as if on cue his father's colors burst from across the meadow and enveloped him. He was lost in a wash of ruby and vermillion, magenta and violet, as the light and color whirled around and embraced him. And somehow, in the middle of the exploding storm, he found himself running across the meadow to find his father, running toward the source of the colors and emotions. He was a little boy wanting his daddy, and for the first time he was not afraid. He was running, not caring for anything but the object of his heart, and he found him. His father was on his knees awash in light, tears sparkling like a waterfall of diamonds and jewels into the hands that covered his face.

"Daddy!" yelled Mack, and he threw himself onto the man who could not even look at his son. In the howl of wind and flame, Mack took his father's face in his two hands, forcing his dad to look him in the face so he could stammer the words he had always wanted to say: "Daddy, I'm so sorry! Daddy, I love you!" The light of his words seemed to blast darkness out of his father's colors, turning them bloodred. They exchanged sobbing words of confession and forgiveness, as a love greater than either one healed them.

6. **Reflect on forgiveness, healing, and restoration in this passage and in your own life. (Do not force anything, just be honest with yourself and God.)**

WITH ARMS AROUND each other they listened, unable to speak through the tears, to the song of reconciliation that lit the night sky. An arching fountain of brilliant color began among the children, especially those who had suffered the greatest, and then rippled as if passed from one to the next by the wind, until the entire field was flooded with light and song.

Mack somehow knew that this was not a time for conversation and that his time with his father was quickly passing. He sensed that by some mystery this was as much for his dad as it was for him. As for Mack, the new lightness he felt was euphoric.

7. Reflections.

THE ANTICIPATION WAS palpable. Suddenly to their right, and from out of the darkness emerged Jesus, and pandemonium broke out. He was dressed in a simple brilliant white garment and wore on his head a simple gold crown, but he was every inch the King of the universe.

8. Reflect on seeing with "healed eyes" the King of the universe.

...THE CENTER OF all creation, the man who is God and the God who is man. Light and color danced and wove a tapestry of love for him to step on. Some were crying out words of love, while others simply stood with hands lifted up. Many of those whose colors were the richest and deepest were lying flat on their faces. Everything that had a breath sang out a song of unending love and thankfulness. Tonight the universe was as it was intended.

9. Reflect on worship and the universe as it was intended.

As JESUS REACHED the center he paused to look around. His gaze stopped on Mack standing on the small hill at the outer edge, and he heard Jesus whisper in his ear, "Mack, I am especially fond of you." That was all Mack could bear as he slumped to the ground, dissolving into a wash of joyful tears. He couldn't move, gripped as he was in Jesus' embrace of love and tenderness.

10. Have you ever heard, or at least longed for, this whisper deep in your heart? What was the experience like?

A MORNING OF SORROWS

Trusting the Loving Presence of God in the Valley of the Shadow of Death

An infinite God can give all of Himself to each of His children.
He does not distribute Himself that each may have a part, but to each
one He gives all of Himself as fully as if there were no others.
—A. W. TOZER

1. Reflect on having all God's attention.

THE MAN STANDING next to him looked a bit like Papa; dignified, older, wiry, and taller than Mack. He had silver-white hair pulled back into a ponytail, matched by a gray-splashed mustache and goatee. Plaid shirt with sleeves rolled up, jeans, and hiking boots completed the outfit of someone ready to hit the trail. "Papa?" Mack asked.

"Yes, son."

Mack shook his head. "You're still messing with me, aren't you?"

"Always," he said with a warm smile, and then answered Mack's next question before it was asked. "This morning you're going to need a father."

2. Reflect on God being what you need.

"**Nothing is a** ritual, Mackenzie."

3. **This statement has been made several times throughout** *The Shack*. **Reflect on religious ritual in your relationship with God.**

"**You really love** him, don't you? Jesus, I mean."

"I know who you mean," Papa answered, laughing. He paused in the middle of washing the fry pan. "With all of my heart! I suppose there is something very special about an only begotten Son." Papa winked at Mack and continued. "That is part of the uniqueness in which I know him."

4. **Reflect on Christ and relationship within the Trinity.**

As they hiked, Mack thought about the myriad of things he had experienced during the previous two days. The conversations with each of the three, alone and then together, the time with Sophia, the devotion he had been part of, looking at the night sky with Jesus, the walk across the lake. And then last night's celebration topped it off, including the reconciliation with his father—so much healing with so little spoken. It was hard to take it all in.

5. **Reflect on your time with God in** *The Shack*. **Has it been healing? Why or why not? Intellectually, it all may not make sense right now, but reflect on the changes deep inside that may be hard to put into words.**

HE KNEW ONLY that he would never be the same again and wondered what these changes would mean for Nan and him and the kids, especially Kate.

6. How has your experience with God changed things in and around you?

"I UNDERSTAND, MACKENZIE. We are coming full circle. Forgiving your dad yesterday was a significant part of your being able to know me as Father today."

7. Is there some aspect of God that is hard for you to comprehend, accept, or relate to? Why or why not?

"THERE WAS NO way to create freedom without a cost, as you know." Papa looked down, scars visible and indelibly written into his wrists. "I knew that my creation would rebel, would choose independence and death, and I knew what it would cost me to open a path of reconciliation. Your independence has unleashed what seems to you a world of chaos, random and frightening. Could I have prevented what happened to Missy? The answer is yes."

Mack looked up at Papa, his eyes asking the question that didn't need voicing. Papa continued, "First, by not creating at all, these questions would be moot. Or second, I could have chosen to actively interfere in her circumstance. The first was never a consideration, and the latter was not an option for purposes that you cannot possibly understand now. At this point, all I have to offer you as an answer are my love and goodness, and my relationship with you. I did not purpose Missy's death, but that doesn't mean I can't use it for good."

8. Can you accept this answer from God? Why or why not?

MACK SHOOK HIS head sadly. "You're right. I don't grasp it very well. I think I see a glimpse for a second and then all the longing and loss I feel seems to rise up and tell me that what I thought I saw just couldn't be true. But I do trust you..." And suddenly, it was like a new thought, surprising and wonderful. "Papa, I *do* trust you!"

9. Can you trust God even in your hurt, anger, doubt, fear, and pain?

HE APPEARED TROUBLED. "I want to show you something that is going to be very painful for you.... To help you see it, I want to take away one more thing that darkens your heart."

10. Reflect on what this is like for Mack. Has God ever said these words to you? Write down your conversation with God about it.

PAPA SPOKE GENTLY and reassuringly. "Son, this is not about shaming you. I don't do humiliation, or guilt, or condemnation. They don't produce one speck of wholeness or righteousness, and that is why they were nailed into Jesus on the cross."

11. Does your god do humiliation, guilt, and condemnation? Does God do humiliation, guilt, and condemnation? What is the difference between your internalized, self-critical voice (your god) and God?

"TODAY WE ARE on a healing trail to bring closure to this part of your journey—not just for you, but for others as well. Today, we are throwing a big rock into the lake, and the resulting ripples will reach places you would not expect. You already know what I want, don't you?"

"I'm afraid I do," Mack mumbled, feeling emotions rising as they seeped out of a locked room in his heart.

"Son, you need to speak it, to name it."

12. **Are there deep things that you have buried away, things that you need to speak to God, others, and yourself?**

NOW THERE WAS no holding back as hot tears poured down his face, and between sobs Mack cried, "Papa, how can I ever forgive that son of a bitch who killed my Missy? If he were here today, I don't know what I would do. I know it isn't right, but I want him to hurt like he hurt me...If I can't get justice, I still want revenge."

Papa simply let the torrent rush out of Mack, waiting for the wave to pass.

"Mack, for you to forgive this man is for you to release him to me and allow me to redeem him."

"Redeem him?" Again Mack felt the fire of anger and hurt. "I don't want you to redeem him! I want you to hurt him, to punish him, to put him in hell..." His voice trailed off.

13. **Reflect on Mack's demand, and possibly your own, for justice or at least revenge.**

"I'M STUCK, PAPA. I can't just forget what he did, can I?" Mack implored.

"Forgiveness is not about forgetting, Mack. It is about letting go of another person's throat."

14. What makes forgiveness so hard?

"BUT I THOUGHT you forgot our sins."

"Mack, I am God. I forgot nothing. I know everything. So forgetting for me is the choice to limit myself. Son"—Papa's voice got quiet and Mack looked up at him, directly into his deep brown eyes—"because of Jesus, there is now no law demanding that I bring your sins back to mind. They are gone when it comes to you and me, and they run no interference in our relationship."

"But this man..."

"But he too is my son. I want to redeem him."

"So what then? I just forgive him and everything is okay, and we become buddies?" Mack stated softly but sarcastically.

"You don't have a relationship with this man, at least not yet. Forgiveness does not establish relationship. In Jesus, I have forgiven all humans for their sins against me, but only some choose relationship."

15. Reflect on forgiveness, forgetting, and relationship.

"MACKENZIE, DON'T YOU see that forgiveness is an incredible power—a power you share with us, a power Jesus gives to all he indwells so that reconciliation can grow? When Jesus forgave those who nailed him to the cross they were no longer in his debt, nor mine. In my relationship with those men, I will never bring up what they did or shame them or embarrass them."

16. Reflect on the power of forgiveness and reconciliation.

"I DON'T THINK I can do this," Mack whispered.

"I want you to. Forgiveness is first for you, the forgiver," answered Papa, "to release you from something that will eat you alive, that will destroy your joy and your ability to love fully and openly. Do you think this man cares about the pain and torment you have gone through? If anything, he feeds on that knowledge. Don't you want to cut that off? And in doing so, you'll release him from a burden that he carries whether he knows it or not—acknowledges it or not. When you choose to forgive another, you love him well."

17. **Are there individuals in your life who are hard to forgive? Take some time to have your own conversation with Papa about forgiveness.**

"I DO NOT love him."

"Not today, you don't. But I do, Mack, not for what he's become, but for the broken child that has been twisted by his pain. I want to help you take on that nature that finds more power in love and forgiveness than hate."

18. **Let yourself reflect deeply on your own life and interactions with others. How quickly do you turn to anger, resentment, possibly even hate? Reflect on the power of anger and hate versus the power of love and forgiveness.**

"MACKENZIE," PAPA WAS strong and firm. "I already told you that forgiveness does not create a relationship. Unless people speak the truth about what they have done and change their minds and behavior, a relationship of trust is not possible. When you forgive someone you certainly release him from judgment, but without true change, no real relationship can be established."

"So forgiveness does not require me to pretend what he did never happened?"

"How can you? You forgave your dad last night. Will you ever forget what he did to you?"

"I don't think so."

"But now you can love him in the face of it. His change allows for that. Forgiveness in no way requires that you trust the one you forgive. But should they finally confess and repent, you will discover a miracle in your own heart that allows you to reach out and begin to build between you a bridge of reconciliation."

19. **Is there anyone in your life that you need to forgive but cannot and maybe should not trust yet? Reflect on forgiveness and maintaining healthy boundaries. Remember that forgiveness is largely to free you the forgiver. What about reconciliation with this person? Remember, reconciliation is an arduous two-way journey of rebuilding trust that is neither required nor expected of the offended. As you reflect on this individual, let Papa help you sort out forgiveness and reconciliation issues deep within you.**

"PAPA, I THINK I understand what you're saying. But it feels like if I forgive this guy he gets off free. How do I excuse what he did? Is it fair to Missy if I don't stay angry with him?"

"Mackenzie, forgiveness does not excuse anything. Believe me, the last thing this man is, is free. And you have no duty to justice in this. I will handle that."

20. **Reflections.**

"AS FOR MISSY, she has already forgiven him."

"She has?" Mack didn't even look up. "How could she?"

"Because of my presence in her. That's the only way true forgiveness is ever possible."

Mack felt Papa sit down next to him on the ground, but he still didn't look up. As Papa's arms enfolded Mack he began to cry. "Let it all out," he heard Papa whisper, and he finally was able to do just that. He closed his eyes as the tears poured out. Missy and her memories again flooded his mind: visions of coloring books and crayons and torn and bloody dresses. He wept until he had cried out all the darkness, all the longing, and all the loss, until there was nothing left.

With his eyes now closed, rocking back and forth, he pleaded, "Help me, Papa. Help me! What do I do? How do I forgive him?"

"Tell him."

21. **Allow God's presence to embrace you and help you to forgive. Reflections.**

PAPA HELD HIM close. "Mackenzie, you are such a joy."

22. **You may never have considered the possibility of a loving God before, but let yourself slip into this embrace. Reflect on the experience.**

"SO IS IT all right if I'm still angry?"

Papa was quick to respond. "Absolutely! What he did was terrible. He caused incredible pain to many. It was wrong, and anger is the right response to something that is so wrong. But don't let the anger and pain and loss you feel prevent you from forgiving him and removing your hands from around his neck."

Papa grabbed his pack and threw it on. "Son, you may have to declare your forgiveness a hundred times the first day and the second day, but the third day will be less and each day after, until one day you will realize that you have forgiven completely."

23. Reflect on anger, forgiveness, and letting go of someone's throat.

SUDDENLY IT ALL made sense. He looked at Sarayu's gift and realized what it was for. Somewhere in this desolate landscape the killer had hidden Missy's body and they had come to retrieve it.... Mack couldn't help but laugh, which seemed so out of place, but then on second thought he knew it was perfect. It was a laugh of hope and restored joy...of the process of closure.

24. Reflect on what you have lost or what decay and destruction have taken from you. Reflect on the healing process God has brought you through so far. What are the next steps that need to happen for you to have true closure?

IT TOOK THEM only a few minutes to find their bittersweet treasure. On a small rock outcropping, Mack saw the body of what he assumed was his Missy; faceup, her body covered by a dirty and decaying sheet. He knew that, like an old glove without a hand to animate it, the real Missy wasn't there.

Papa unwrapped what Sarayu had sent with them and immediately the den filled with wonderful living aromas and scents. Even though the sheet under Missy's body was fragile, it held enough for Mack to lift her and place her in the midst of all the flowers and spices. Papa then tenderly wrapped her up and carried her to the entrance.

25. If you have traumatic memories of death, decay, and loss, take time to go on this journey with God and let him wrap the decay in his presence and the sweet aromas from the garden of your heart.

CHOICES OF THE HEART

Planting a Tree of Life and Choosing to Live for What Matters

Earth has no sorrow that Heaven cannot heal.
—THOMAS MOORE

1. Reflections.

JESUS GENTLY RELIEVED him of his burden and together they went to the shop where he had been working.... Directly before them stood his work, a masterpiece of art in which to lay the remains of Missy. As Mack walked around the box he immediately recognized the etchings in the wood. On closer examination he discovered that details of Missy's life were carved into the wood. He found an engraving of Missy with her cat, Judas. There was another of Mack sitting in a chair reading Dr. Seuss to her. All the family was visible in scenes worked into the sides and top: Nan and Missy making cookies, the trip to Wallowa Lake with the tram ascending the mountain, and even Missy coloring at the camp table along with an accurate representation of the ladybug pin the killer had left behind. There was even an accurate rendering of Missy standing and smiling as she looked into the waterfall, knowing her daddy was on the other side. Interspersed throughout were flowers and animals that were Missy's favorites.

Mack turned and hugged Jesus, and as they embraced, Jesus whispered into his ear, "Missy helped—she picked out what she wanted on it."

2. **Reflect on what is going on at this stage of the healing process in Mack's life and possibly your own.**

"WE HAVE THE perfect place prepared for her body," Sarayu said, sweeping past. "Mackenzie, it is in *our* garden."

With great care they gently placed the remains of Missy into the box, laying her on a bed of soft grasses and moss, and then filled it full with the flowers and spices from Sarayu's pack. Closing the lid, Jesus and Mack each easily picked up an end and carried it out, following Sarayu into the garden to the place in the orchard that Mack had helped clear. There, between cherry and peach trees, surrounded by orchids and daylilies, a hole had been dug right where Mack had uprooted the flowering shrub the day before.

3. **Reflect on this burial in Mack's heart and how it is different than *The Great Sadness*.**

SARAYU STEPPED FORWARD. "I," she said with a flourish and bow, "am honored to sing Missy's song, which she wrote just for this occasion."

4. **Possibly through reading this chapter the Holy Spirit is singing you the song of someone you have lost. Reflect on that experience or at least reflect on the idea of the Holy Spirit singing us the song of those whom we have lost.**

WHEN THE TASK was complete, Sarayu reached within her clothing and withdrew her small, fragile bottle. From it she poured out a few drops of the precious collection into her hand and began to carefully scatter Mack's tears onto the rich black soil under which Missy's body slept. The droplets fell like diamonds and rubies, and wherever they landed flowers instantly burst upward and bloomed in the brilliant sun. Sarayu then paused for a moment, looking intently at one pearl resting in her hand, a special tear, and then dropped it into the center of the plot. Immediately a small tree broke through the earth and began unbending itself from the spot, young and luxurious and stunning, growing and maturing until it burst into blossom and bloom. Sarayu then, in her whispery breeze-blown way, turned and smiled at Mack, who had been watching transfixed. "It is a tree of life, Mack, growing in the garden of your heart."

5. Reflections.

PAPA SMILED. "WE are especially fond of you, you know. But here is the choice for you to make. You can remain with us and continue to grow and learn, or you can return to your other home, to Nan and to your children and friends. Either way, we promise to always be with you, although this way is a little more overt and obvious."

...Finally, Mack asked, "What would Missy want?"

"Although she would love to be with you today, she lives where there is no impatience. She does not mind waiting."

"I'd love to be with her." He smiled at the thought. "But this would be so hard on Nan and my other children. Let me ask you something. Is what I do back home important? Does it matter? I really don't do much other than working and caring for my family and friends—"

Sarayu interrupted him. "Mack, if anything matters then everything matters. Because you are important, everything you do is important. Every time you forgive, the universe changes; every time you reach out and touch a heart or a life, the world changes; with every kindness and service, seen or unseen, my purposes are accomplished and nothing will ever be the same again."

6. **Reflect on wanting to be with Jesus and those whom you have lost. What would you choose? What do you still have to do that matters?**

"I KNOW THAT I can make some difference, no matter how little that difference might be. There are a few things I need, uh, want to do anyway."

7. **Why did Mack catch himself and change "need" to "want to do"?**

"AND I REALLY do believe that you will never leave me or abandon me, so I am not afraid to go back. Well, maybe a little."

8. **As you walk forward into the rest of your life, reflect on God never leaving or abandoning you.**

NOW SARAYU STOOD in front of Mack and spoke. "Mackenzie, now that you are going back, I have one more gift for you to take."

"What is it?" Mack asked, curious about anything that Sarayu might give.

"It is for Kate," she said.

"Kate?" exclaimed Mack, realizing that he still carried her as a burden in his heart. "Please, tell me."

"Kate believes that she is to blame for Missy's death."

Mack was stunned. What Sarayu had told him was so obvious. It made perfect sense that Kate would blame herself. She had raised the paddle that started the sequence of events that led to Missy's being taken. He couldn't believe the thought had never even crossed his mind. In one moment, Sarayu's words opened a new vista into Kate's struggle.

9. **Reflect on the gift of the Holy Spirit's insight into the heart of someone you care about. How does that impact the relationship?**

FINALLY, JESUS STOOD and reached up to one of the shelves to bring down Mack's little tin box. "Mack, I thought you might want this..."

Mack took it from Jesus and held it in his hands a moment. "Actually, I don't think I'm going to need this anymore," he said. "Can you keep it for me? All my best treasures are now hidden in you anyway. I want you to be my life."

"I am," came the clear and true voice of assurance.

10. **Reflections.**

"GOD, THE SERVANT." He chuckled but then felt a welling-up again as the thought made him pause. "It is more truly God, my servant."

11. **Reflect. How has God taken care of you?**

HE WAS BACK in the real world. Then he smiled to himself. It was more likely he was back in the un-real world.

12. Reflect on this statement and the day-to-day world you live in.

HE WAS ANXIOUS to get home to his family, especially Kate.

Lost in thought, Mack simply pulled through the intersection when the light turned green. He never even saw the other driver run the opposing red light. There was only a brilliant flash of light and then nothing, except silence and inky blackness.

In a split second Willie's red Jeep was destroyed, in minutes Fire and Rescue and the police arrived, and within hours Mack's broken and unconscious body was delivered by Life Flight to Emmanuel Hospital in Portland, Oregon.

13. Reflections.

OUTBOUND RIPPLES

Coming Out of a Coma and Letting Others See the Real You

Faith never knows where it is being led,
but it knows and loves the One who is leading.
—OSWALD CHAMBERS

1. Reflections.

ONE AFTER ANOTHER, a parade of people rushed up to his one barely open eye, as if they were looking into a deep dark hole containing some incredible treasure. Whatever they saw seemed to please them immensely, and off they would go to spread the news.

Some faces he recognized, but the ones he didn't, Mack soon learned, were those of his doctors and nurses. He slept often, but it seemed that every time he opened his eyes it would cause no little excitement. *Just wait until I can stick out my tongue,* he thought. *That will really get them.*

2. You may want to reflect on what Mack and his family are going through here, or consider spending time reflecting on those people who cross your path, those people who look deep into your eyes hoping to glimpse the real you that they treasure.

3. After reading *The Shack*, you may realize you have been dealing with your own *Great Sadness*. Even now as God has joined you to bring healing to your heart, you may find that your body is in your own kind of coma. In this chapter, reflect on how you can come out of it and let others who delight in you see more of the "real" you.

HE VAGUELY REMEMBERED the drive to the shack, but things got sketchy beyond that. In his dreams the images of Papa, Jesus, Missy playing by the lake, Sophia in the cave, and the light and color of the festival in the meadow came back to him like shards from a broken mirror. Each was accompanied by waves of delight and joy, but he wasn't sure if they were real or hallucinations conjured up by collisions between some damaged or otherwise wayward neurons and the drugs coursing through his veins.

4. Reflect again on what is "real" in the world. What things sometimes get in the way and confuse or cause you to question your experience with God?

MACK SMILED AS he listened to Willie rant. If he had few other memories, he did remember this man cared about him and just having him near made him smile. Mack was suddenly startled to realize that Willie had leaned down very close to his face.

"Seriously, was *he* there?" he whispered, then quickly looked around to make sure no one was within ear shot.

5. Who makes you smile just having them near? Who believes your experiences with God even when you're not sure yourself? Take time to talk with them about things deep inside you this week.

THAT'S WHEN THE penny dropped and the disjointed story began to crystallize in Mack's mind. Everything suddenly made sense as his mind began connecting the dots and filling in the details—the note, the Jeep, the gun, the trip to the shack, and every facet of that glorious weekend. The images and memories began to flood back so powerfully that he felt as if they might pick him up and sweep him off his bed and out of this world. And as he remembered he began to cry, until tears were rolling down his cheeks.

"Mack, I'm sorry." Willie was now begging and apologetic. "What did I say?"

Mack reached up and touched his friend's face. "Nothing, Willie. I remember everything now. The note, the shack, Missy, Papa. I remember everything."

6. **Remember and share all of what you have experienced with God through this study. (Share at your own pace in trusted relationships. If you don't have a Willie in your life, trust that Papa will lead you to one.)**

"OH, YEAH," HE said at last. "He told me to tell you something."

"What? Me?" Mack watched as concern and doubt traded places on Willie's face. "So, what did he say?" Again he leaned forward.

Mack paused, grasping for the words. "He said, 'Tell Willie that I'm especially fond of him.'"

Start looking for your Willie by listening for who Papa tells you he is especially fond of.

AS SHE TALKED, Mack thought it indeed strange that he would get in an accident right after spending a weekend with God. *The seemingly random chaos of life,* wasn't that how Papa put it?

7. Reflect on your expectations of life after your healing and growing experiences with God.

WHEN NAN FINISHED recounting her side of the events, Mack began telling her all that had happened to him. But first, he asked for her forgiveness, confessing how and why he had lied to her. This surprised Nan, and she credited his new transparency to the trauma and morphine.

8. As you begin to move forward and share your story, reflect on who you may need to ask forgiveness from. Ask God to join you in writing out some thoughts that need to be said to this individual.

THE FULL STORY of his weekend, or day as Nan kept reminding him, unfolded slowly, spread over a number of different tellings. Sometimes the drugs would get the better of him and he would slip off to dreamless sleep, occasionally mid-sentence. Initially, Nan focused on being patient and attentive, trying as best she could to suspend judgment but not seriously considering that his ravings were anything but remnants of neurological damage.

But the vividness and depth of his memories touched her and slowly undermined her resolve to stay objective. There was life in what he was telling her, and she quickly understood that whatever had happened had greatly impacted and changed her husband.

9. **It may be hard to share your story coherently at first, but trust that "there is life" in it and that life, his life, will shine through. Some will see that life, some will not. Reflect on your attempts so far at sharing your story from your shack experiences.**

"I **WANT TO** talk to you about Missy."

Kate jerked back as if stung by a yellow jacket, her face turning dark. Instinctively she tried to pull her hand away, but Mack held tight, which took a considerable portion of his strength. She glanced around. Nan came up and put her arm around her. Kate was trembling. "Why?" she demanded in a whisper.

"Katie, it wasn't your fault."

Now she hesitated, almost as if she had been caught with a secret. "What's not my fault?"

Again, it took effort to get the words out, but she clearly heard. "That we lost Missy." Tears rolled down his cheeks as he struggled with those simple words.

Again she recoiled, turning away from him.

"Honey, no one blames you for what happened."

Her silence lasted only a few seconds longer before the dam burst. "But if I hadn't been careless in the canoe, you wouldn't have had to..." Her voice filled with self-loathing.

Mack interrupted with a hand on her arm. "That's what I'm trying to tell you, honey. It's not your fault."

Kate sobbed as her father's words penetrated her war-ravaged heart.

"But I've always thought it was my fault. And I thought that you and Mom blamed me, and I didn't mean..."

"None of us meant for this to happen, Kate. It just happened, and we'll learn to live through it. But we'll learn together. Okay?"

10. There may be those you need to share your story with, who like Nan will see the life in it. There will be others who, because of your time with Papa in your shack, you will have an opportunity to speak life into, like Kate. Reflect on knowing and being known, seeing the life of Jesus in one another, and learning to live through it together.

WHEN NAN NOTICED that his eyes had opened, she quietly approached so as not to wake their daughter and kissed him. "I believe you," she whispered, and he nodded and smiled, surprised by how important that was to hear.

11. Reflect on being believed and being believed in.

12. Reflect on the last two pages of this chapter. During your time with Papa, you may have received clues about how to bring closure to some things in your life. Reflect on these things and talk to Sarayu about the guidance and support you may still need.

AFTER WORDS

Your Healing Journey

Our Shack experiences can be scared and sacred space;
it is all in how you "C."

AS FOR MACK, he continues to live his normal productive life and remains adamant that every word of the story is true. All the changes in his life, he tells me, are enough evidence for him. *The Great Sadness* is gone and he experiences most days with a profound sense of joy.

So the question I am faced with as I pen these words is, how to end a tale like this? Perhaps I can do that best by telling you a little about how it has affected me. As I stated in the foreword, Mack's story changed me. I don't think that there is one aspect of my life, especially my relationships, that hasn't been touched deeply and altered in ways that truly matter. Do I think it's true? I want all of it to be true. Perhaps if some of it is not actually true in one sense, it is still true nonetheless—if you know what I mean. I guess you and Sarayu will have to figure that one out.

1. **Reflect on your shack experiences. How have they impacted you and those around you not just as individuals, but how have they impacted relationships?**

AND MACK? WELL, he's a human being who continues through a process of change like the rest of us. Only he welcomes it while I tend to resist it. I have noticed that he loves larger than most, is quick to forgive and even quicker to ask for forgiveness. The transformations in him have caused quite a ripple through his community of relationships—and not all of them easy. But I have to tell you that I've never been around another adult who lives life with such simplicity and joy. Somehow he has become a child again. Or maybe more accurately, he's become the child he never was allowed to be, abiding in simple trust and wonder. He embraces even the darker shades of life as part of some incredibly rich and profound tapestry crafted masterfully by invisible hands of love.

2. **If you have experienced growth, healing, and life transformation through your time with Papa in *The Shack*, please understand that life is still life. The process of change continues. Welcome it, and may you always feel and know the embrace of Papa, Sarayu, and Jesus. Reflections.**

IF YOU EVER get a chance to hang out with Mack, you will soon learn that he's hoping for a new revolution, one of love and kindness—a revolution that revolves around Jesus and what he did for us all and what he continues to do in anyone who has a hunger for reconciliation and a place to call home. This is not a revolution that will overthrow anything, or if it does, it will do so in ways we could never contrive in advance. Instead, it will be the quiet daily powers of dying and serving and loving and laughing, of simple tenderness and unseen kindness, because *if anything matters, then everything matters*. And one day, when all is revealed, every one of us will bow our knees and confess in the power of Sarayu that Jesus is the Lord of all creation, to the glory of Papa.

3. **Reflect on your hunger for reconciliation and a place to call home.**

4. **After your time with Papa, you may feel energized for action. Reflect one last time on expectancy and responsiveness versus expectations and responsibilities, and enjoy the invitation to the daily powers of dying and serving and loving and laughing, of simple tenderness and unseen kindness.**

CONTINUE YOUR EXPERIENCE WITH *THE SHACK*

We invite you to continue your experience with *The Shack* at our website: WmPaulYoung.com.

- Share how you feel about *The Shack* and read what others are saying.
- Communicate with the author.
- Purchase additional copies of *The Shack*.

For information about having the authors speak to your organization or group, please contact Wes Yoder at (615) 370-4700, Ext. 230, or Wes@AmbassadorSpeakers.com.

CONTACT WM. PAUL YOUNG

Is it possible to craft a space for community and conversation free of the divisiveness of politics and religion and ideology...a space to explore life, God, the world, and what it is to be fully human, alongside a growing group of friends?

I would love to try. If that sounds like something you're interested in, join the ever unfolding conversation about God, life, and the world at:

WmPaulYoung.com

Or write to me at:

Paul Young
PO Box 2107
Oregon City, OR 97045
USA

For management inquiries, please contact:

Dan Polk at Baxter/Stinson/Polk LLC at www.bspequity.com

To schedule speaking engagements, please contact:

Ambassador Speakers Bureau at Info@AmbassadorSpeakers.com

About the Authors

Wm. Paul Young

Wm. Paul Young is the author of *The Shack*, which has sold over twenty million copies worldwide, and the novels *Cross Roads* and *Eve*. He was born a Canadian and along with three younger siblings was raised among a Stone Age tribe by his missionary parents in the highlands of what was New Guinea (West Papua). The family returned to Canada where his father pastored a number of churches for various denominations. By the time he entered Canadian Bible College, Paul had attended a dozen schools. He completed his undergraduate degree in religion at Warner Pacific College in Portland, Oregon. He suffered great loss as a child and young adult, and now enjoys the "wastefulness of grace" with his family in the Pacific Northwest.

Brad Robison M.D.

Brad Robison M.D. is a psychiatrist who has been in private practice for twenty years in Cape Girardeau, Missouri, where he has joined God in creating sacred space for countless individuals and families. He has been a part of starting Sacred Space Ministries, whose mission is to develop intensive spiritual growth and life transformation experiences for individuals, families, and groups, including Sacred Space Trauma Recovery (livesacredspace. org or Facebook). Dr. Robison has been married to his wife, Paula, for thirty years. He has joined her with delight as God has created and refined the sacred space of family in and through them for their three children.

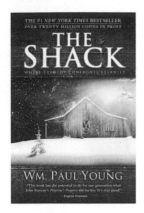

THE SHACK

Mackenzie Allen Phillips's youngest daughter, Missy, has been abducted during a family vacation, and evidence that she may have been brutally murdered is found in an abandoned shack deep in the Oregon wilderness. Four years later, in this midst of his great sadness, Mack receives a suspicious note, apparently from God, inviting him back to that shack for a weekend.

Against his better judgment, he arrives at the shack on wintry afternoon and walks back into his darkest nightmare. What he finds there will change his life forever.

THE SHACK REVISITED

Continue your experience with *The Shack Revisited* by C. Baxter Kruger (foreword by Wm. Paul Young), the book that guides readers into a deeper understanding of God the Father, God the Son, and God the Holy Spirit, to help readers have a more profound connection with the core message of *The Shack*—God is love.

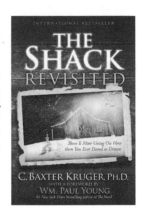

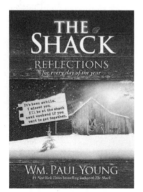

THE SHACK REFLECTIONS

This 365-day devotional selects meaningful quotes from *The Shack* and adds prayers by writer Wm. Paul Young to inspire, encourage, and uplift you every day of the year.

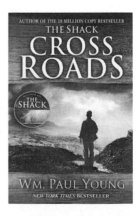

CROSS ROADS

Wm. Paul Young, author of the international bestseller *The Shack*, tells a story of the incremental transformation of a man caught in the torments of his own creation, somewhere between heaven and earth.